A Year Down North

William Richard Matheson

ACKNOWLEDGEMENTS

COVER PHOTOGRAPH: CREDIT: NWT Archives/Sacred Heart Parish(Fort Simpson) fonds/N-1992-255: 0014
AUTHOR PHOTOGRAPH: Courtesy Global TV Edmonton, Alberta

DEDICATION

For Kit

Forward

Most Canadians live within two hundred miles of the country's southern border. The rest of the country, stretching all the way to the North Pole, is for the most part, left alone. One winter in the late 1940's the temperature at Snag, in the Yukon territory, went down to 80 degrees below zero Fahrenheit. One's breath didn't just condense, it froze upon exhalation, and anyone venturing outside had a small snowstorm, precipitating just under one's nose. In the summertime, the heat in the territories can become oppressive, warmer by far than along the St. Lawrence river or the Pacific Coast. This heat nurtures limitless galaxies of flies that seem as numerous as the molecules of air. A strange country: As if it were of extra-terrestrial origin and hadn't yet fit into the earth's scheme of things. A vast, trackless forest on one side, riven by massive lakes and mighty rivers; on the other side a flat, featureless waste of cold rock where life ventures timidly; the ice might come again to carry off every living thing and destroy the soil. Strange country: Where the sun stays up half the year, and vanishes for the other half, replaced by the eerie fantasy of the northern lights, glowing curtains billowing across the star-strewn blackness of space. People are not wanted here. You'll not find brand Excalibur lunging from these lakes, and no ghostly echoes steal down from the Mackenzie Mountains, which may be why Canadian heroes are always running afoul of their environment. They are forever freezing to death, drowning, eaten up by bears or wolves, falling from cliffs, starving in the wilderness, going mad from loneliness, of the predations of the "no see-um" flies. For every Samuel Hearne, there are scores of wretches from the lost Franklin Expedition, gone forever and leaving no shades behind.

Fort Poontuk is my fictional settlement on the Mackenzie River. Seen from the air, (and since there were no roads, rail or otherwise into the place, one always saw it first from the air) it appeared not so much strange, as ridiculous: What was it doing down there? For countless miles around there was nothing but the forest, and here on a tiny cleared enclave on the river, was the haphazard collection of buildings. Closer inspection yielded an Anglican Church, with a steeple, a tin-sheathed Catholic hospital, a scattering of log "but-and-bens", some in good condition, most of them ramshackle.

Communication with the "Outside", as anywhere south of the territories is known, was maintained by the now defunct Royal Canadian Corps of Signals.[1]

Human nature, whatever it is, doesn't change much. The railings of Plato against the young bloods of his day are as applicable now as then, and any society, despite the strictures of its particular religion or code of moral conduct, always has its share of scoundrels and saints, leaders and madmen. There remain the startling differences in various cultures' approaches to social intercourse, manners if you will, which must be accounted to something. The half-naked, primitive woman who squeezes her breast and offers it as a gesture of friendship is, heaven help us, acting in a somewhat different manner than a Victorian society matron, trussed up in stays, who asks the visitor if he wants one lump or two in his tea. The Restoration dandy, who with his elaborate curtsies, follows a pattern in keeping with frills and laces, furbelows and powdered periwig, is a species apart from the finance company manager with his grey sack suit and button

---

[1] For more information about the signalmen and their contribution to northern communications and electronics the reader is referred to the following excellent website: http://www.nwtandy.rcsigs.ca . The Royal Canadian Corps of Signals was established in 1903 as the first independent signal corps of the British Empire. The corps was renamed the Royal Canadian Corps of Signals in 1922, and was a branch of the Canadian army, and then the Canadian armed forces. In 1947, just after the Second World War, the time of this story, there were 23 northern stations in operation. In 1959 the stations were transferred to civilian hands under the Department of Transportation.

down collar.

Ascribe the difference to costume and don't worry too much about what brings about the ever-changing panorama of fashion. In dealing with Poontukians, we are looking at persons whose costume was more a matter of dictation than choice; a response to fiats issued by a climate that accepts or countenances no compromise. In the wintertime, all Poontukians were forced into heavy, sensible clothing, and it appeared that their relationships one to the other were the same; without artifice. No nonsense in costume lead to no nonsense in manners: Get along, compromise, there are the shibboleths that stamp the manners of the northerner, and point-up the cool, easy going mien of Canadians in general. Bluebooks and social distinctions imported from other countries find little welcome in Canada, and this causes foreign observers to wonder at the lack of patriotism coupled with the bewildering search for national identity. The mid-summer visitor from lower latitudes, who arrives with a fur coat and snowshoes in Winnipeg and Montreal is reacting to an impression from abroad that the placid, not to say resigned manner of Canadians must be brought about by elements of nature so harsh that it is with amazement the visitor learns that some people live in Canada all year round. It may all be nonsense, but the Canadian penchant for compromise, reflected in a string of mind-numbing Acts of Parliament rather than conflict and bloodshed, is the dominant feature. Injustice, bigotry and discrimination abound as elsewhere, but these are papered over by historians who, in dealing with them at all, do so with a hand-wringing sense of profound shame. Convicted traitors are resurrected and deified. Injustices visited upon minorities are put down as influences from outside. The Canadian attitude remains: Get along, compromise, because, no matter what, we must stay united against a common enemy, who never grows old and who is nothing if not coquettish.

Chapter 1

Edmonton District Meteorological Offices

The meeting of the District Meteorologist's committee was convened. Seated at the head of the conference table in imposing bulk was the District Meteorologist, known as "the D. Met", Mr. L. Delance Babcock. In a commander, it is proper to have a good psychological distance between him and those he commands, so that there are no qualms when the commander must order his men "over the top" or some equally hazardous enterprise. In this respect, Mr. Babcock was admirably fit: A huge, portly man, towering over his fellows and topped with a shock of fiery red hair, whose effusive color seemed to have invested his cheeks with a rubicund glow and a shower of freckles. Then, too, as a Mormon, Mr. Babcock neither smoked nor drank and woe betide the underling who entered his presence smoking or hung-over.

This corporal rectitude extended to all manner of conduct, and the off-color joke was definitely taboo in Mr. Babcock's intimidating presence. His rectitude however could not withstand his craving for soft drinks and chocolate bars, a penchant that over the years had reduced him to a pear-shaped mass of suet, which seemed permanently stuck to the broad, high backed chair in which he sat. He looked like a non-too-benign Buddha. He took a swig of Coke, munched at a chocolate bar, then slapped his meaty hand on the table.

He spoke: "Let the meeting begin."

Mr. Bodnar, the secretary, arose and distributed the agenda to the others, who represented the meteorological staff, communications, and administrative personnel of the Edmonton Airport offices of the Department of Transport, exercising jurisdiction in meteorological matters over the entire western arctic district.

Mr. Bodnar returned to his chair next to the D. Met.
"You'll notice first of all, Mr. Chairman," he said, "There's been an explosion that destroyed the hydrogen shed at Fort Smith."

"What!" exclaimed the D. Met.

"Yes. It was completely destroyed. I have the radiogram here.." Mr. Bodnar fished about through a voluminous file he raised from the floor. "... ah yes, here it is: 'Hydrogen tank blew up. All equipment and shed completely destroyed. Please advise."

An ominous silence descended over the meeting with the lowering of the great, copper-glinting brows of the D. Met. His green eyes glinted. "Who sent that message?" His voice was slow, fetched up from his bowels.

"Why, it was Meteorological Assistant, Donald Dobbs."

"What!" thundered the D. Met.

The identity of the sender was re-affirmed and the D. Met glowered.

"Just as I suspected. I know that man. A professional skulker, that's what he is. A skulker, gentlemen. He worked here for a time, you know. Oh yes. On every shift he came in a little late, left a little early. Took his coffee break early, left a little late. He's a skulker, do you hear! I sent him up to the weather station at Fort Smith, but if I'd had my way, he would have been at the North Pole. That's right." In his passion, Mr. Babcock had lapsed into a pronounced Mormon accent, the last word came out more precisely as "riot".

He paused. Took a breath. "I suppose there've been no upper air observations since this explosion?"

"No sir," said Mr. Bodner.

"Pardon me," it was one of the forecasters. "But was anyone hurt during the explosion?"

"Ha!" bellowed the D. Met. "I doubt that. Unless I'm

sadly mistaken gentlemen, and I don't think I am.." He paused to allow those about the table to affirm:

"Right you are, Mr. Babcock"

"Yes, Sir", and

"Yes, of course"

"This Dobbs deliberately overloaded the generator so as to cause an explosion. Bodnar, now listen to me. I want Mr. Stewart, the Inspector, to make an immediate investigation of that explosion. Let him leave tomorrow and report directly back to me. In the meantime, have some tanks of hydrogen sent up. That'll fix Mr. Dobbs!"

It was agreed. With a smile, Mr. Bodnar opened the file on the next item of business. The smile vanished. His eyes shifted nervously.

"Well, Bodnar!", goaded the D. Met.

"Well, Sir, it's a matter of some delicacy."

"What!" the D. Met's eyebrows took off again.

"It's about that bursary meteorologist, Mr. Jerome Geoff, sir...he...that is...he was found..."

"Good Lord, man! Speak up. Speak up"

"Well, we've had him plotting weather-maps lately and his work really hasn't been that good, and now he's..."

"Well!" the nuts in the D. Met's chocolate bar that he'd been chewing spewed on the table.

And, like a constipated man suddenly relieved, Bodnar let it flow without let or restraint. "He was found, er, ah, having carnal relations with Angela, the switchboard operator, in the coffee room."

A terrible pause. Then: "What!"

"Well, sir, he was caught fu..."

"Stop!" The D. Met raised his hand, the fingers like links of sausage. "Mr. Bodnar. I want you never to use that word in my presence again. Do you understand."

"Yes, sir."

"Well, go on, tell me more," he said taking a swig of

Coke and fumbling for another chocolate bar.

"Well, Sir, nothing like this has ever happened before. They were found, this Jerome Geoff and Angela, in a state of 'flagrante delicto', I believe the term is. Anyway, they were found out by one of the radio operators, Joe Kleppitz, who threatened to kill Geoff. It seems the girl was Kleppitz's fiancee. He took after Geoff with a knife.."

"The police were called?" the D. Met wanted to know.

"Heavens no, Mr. Babcock," Mr. Bodnar was shocked. "We got them calmed down. I understand they, Geoff and Kleppitz, were rooming together, but Kleppitz has since moved out."

The D. Met thought for a moment. Then he said: "Anymore hanky-panky in the coffee room?"

"Oh, Sir! Of course not. It's just that his work has been most unsatisfactory. I think we should let him go!"

"No, no, " growled the D. Met. "Firing a civil servant these days almost takes an act of parliament. And besides, we can always send him someplace up North, someplace cold and nasty. Wait a minute, I've got it. Didn't that there Cy Trent--that forecaster doing doctoral work on winds at Fort Poontuk -- didn't he put in for an assistant? We could send this lecher up there. Fill Trent's request and get rid of a troublemaker ourselves."

The others agreed. The meeting moved on to the next item on the agenda.

Chapter 2

Young Jerome Geoff

H eironymous (nee Jerome) Geoff's parents had died while he, an only child, was quite young. He'd been brought up in Lethbridge by his Uncle Bert.

Uncle Bert was an energetic Englishman of radical views, who in another day and age might have been marked as a "soldier of fortune" and "rake". Bert had served with the Imperial Army in the First World War and afterward had immigrated to Canada just in time to take part in the General Strike at Winnipeg. Later, he joined the unemployed in the march on Ottawa and was there in Regina during the infamous confrontation with the Mounted Police, when shots were fired and men were killed.

After that, he came back to Lethbridge, but only long enough to pack a bag and hie himself off to Spain, where he joined the International Brigade to fight against France. Returning to Lethbridge again, he joined the veteran's guard when a prisoner-of-war camp was opened there after the outbreak of the Second World War. Bert enlivened his drab existence at the camp by heckling speakers at political rallies. Uncle Bert's experiences in peace and war had left him skeptical of any political party to the right of anarchy. In his view, they were all in the pay of "bloated capitalists, who grind the faces of the poor". Bert never married. He told young Geoff that he never had the time, that his conjugal urges had been "sublimated". Not being subject to the natural constraints of a father, Uncle Bert was able to enthrall his nephew with lengthy and detailed descriptions of what these "sublimations" really meant.

The young Geoff loved and admired his Uncle, a philosopher, raconteur and bon vivant, who'd read everything, been everywhere, and called home where ever he hung his hat. And of course, Uncle Bert had been there when Geoff came bursting through the front door, gasping and breathless because he'd just run about ten miles, to excitedly recount his seeing the Green Flash.

Southern Alberta, in which area Lethbridge is located, enjoys unique natural prerogatives. To the east lie the Cypress Hills, geological anomalies that alone across the southern Canadian prairies were spared the ravages of three ice ages. One imagines them standing isolated in a limitless sea of glittering ice, thrust up and defiant, a kind of ark, nurturing a flora and fauna which to this day are found nowhere else on the prairies. To the west are the blue and white Rockies, home of the Chinook wind, which usurps winter's kingdom to install a premature spring, and then will just as impetuously yield the prize. The real drama of the area is the sky, or more specifically, the air; perfectly clear, like some fantastic lens that at times brings the mountains closer then farther, that responds to the changes wrought by the weather and the sun's passage across the sky. Viewed at intervals throughout the day, one cannot help but feel that the orchestration that produces the violet dawn, the shadowless blaze of noon, and the exuberance of the sunset must be directed by a baton held by God Himself.

Geoff could never remain indifferent to the environment. As he walked on the prairie of the Blood Indian Reserve, which at that time was in its aboriginal, unbroken state, the horizon, if he relaxed and let it happen, would blur and dissolve, yielding to the sky, evanescing more and more so that the only solid ground remaining was that beneath his feet. He would feel the sky move around him, threaten, not threaten, but promise, to swamp that last small patch of ground. And if that remnant should go, he would dissolve in the sky! He would shake off the bounds of time and space. His soul would become one with The One.

One day Geoff had hiked over to the Blood Indian Reservation out of curiosity. A couple of his schoolmates had been hiking in the coulees of the reserve and had made a startling discovery. They'd found the burial grounds of several Indians, who had perished presumably during the smallpox epidemic a half century earlier. The skeletons, wrapped in blankets, lay in open, wooden coffins. His schoolmates wouldn't go back with Geoff. The place was too spooky.

Impatient to discover the grounds for himself, Geoff started out alone. It was a fine summer's morning with scarcely a cloud in the sky when he set out. Later, the cumulus clouds began to build up, and by late afternoon, when Geoff had all but exhausted his patience and energy, a roiling thunderstorm came sweeping down, drenching him to the skin. The storm passed, and the sky cleared as the sun began to decline. Geoff's shadow was stretching to a vanishing point when, cresting the top of still another coulee, he saw them. Below him were the five open coffins.

Cautiously, he descended the coulee, and at the bottom he stopped and looked about. He had an uncanny feeling that he was being watched, and the eyes were not friendly. He moved closer to the coffins. A vagrant ripple of wind brushed through the prairie wood and the words of an old Sunday school tune, sung by a sepulchral choir: "In the waving grass, I see Him pass", for some reason passed through his mind's ear. He stretched his neck to peer over the lip of the coffin.

Someone had torn the skull from the skeleton and smashed it to smithereens. A bony hand had somehow escaped the confines of the blanket.

Then Geoff's blood ran cold. He heard hoof beats. It was a mounted patrol of Indians, he was sure, come to wreak terrible retribution for this desecration.

He stood rooted to the spot for how long he had no idea. But no arrow pierced his heart, no tomahawk was buried in his brain.

He roused himself and looked up. There, etched

against the sky stood a horse and rider. The Indian was looking at him, but remained still as a statue, with plumed spear, decorated shield, and naked but for a breechcloth and moccasins. The wind stirred the feathers in his hair.

Geoff fled blindly down the coulee. But there the path was blocked with a thick copse of bushes, vines and trees, and riven with deep ruts. Carried by feet that suddenly sprouted wings, Geoff flew up the opposite slope of the coulee and reached the top. He stole a quick look around.

The flat prairie stretched away as far as the eye could see. Flat and empty. No rider. The mountains, forty miles away, lay low in a jagged, black-blue line etched against the glowing western sky. No rider there either. Geoff spun about again and again, growing dizzy in the exercise, but horse and rider had vanished.

As the sun sank below the horizon, there came a sudden and distinct change in the sky, as if the sun's touching the horizon had touched some celestial switch. The red glow gathered into a stream and poured itself into the sun, to be replaced by a vibrant blue that shimmered red across the sky in erratic, bright pulsations. The rhythm increased so that it was difficult to watch and reached such frequency as to coalesce into a single, shining pillar of pure emerald light: A shaft that brought the light back to the world and rose up like a searchlight to the very top of the sky. The world turned green, as if the very molecules of the air had been excited. Then the green shaft was gone, as quickly as it had come.

Geoff's senses reeled. He felt he had been granted a special dispensation, a revelation by the gods. Prometheus! No, he had not taken anything, he'd been granted something. He sprinted across the prairie skirting the coulee, leaping and shouting: "I am Ganymede! I am Ganymede!"

There was no money for "Ganymede's" worldly education past the high school level, and Uncle Bert, by dint of connections with the government (after all, he was a veteran of the Two World Wars) arranged for his nephew to write a civil service exam. This landed Geoff in the Department of Transport as a Meteorological Assistant. It is not surprising that Geoff showed a keen interest in atmospheric phenomenon and did so well in subsequent tests that he qualified as a bursary student of meteorology.

At the beginning of his first term at the University of Alberta in Edmonton, Geoff got along reasonably well with his fellow students. All those advanced ideas of his Uncle Bert gave him a head start on most of the students. But Jerome Geoff couldn't adopt a blasé attitude. He was an overweening optimist, a pollyanna.

"We are alive in the greatest age, with the greatest promise of all ages!" he would shout.

He came to be regarded as a bore, a latter day 'Candide', but he never understood. He was too busy delving into the mysteries of his own psyche.

He was aware of a dualism, a Manichean realization within him. When he thought about his Uncle Bert he could not but marvel at the compromise, the peace, the older man had made, since Bert was more aware than most people about the good and evil of this world. But such peace of mind was impossible for Heironymous Geoff, as he now styled himself. He tried the life of a medieval ascetic: He renounced worldly pleasures, denied himself movies, popular books and magazines. He quit jacking-off and studied in-depth the life of St. Paul, fervently hoping that, in his own book-cluttered room, he too might walk his Damascus road. He read voraciously, went as long as he could without sleep, cut out sweets, fasted on Sundays, and gave up beer. For awhile he thought of joining the Mormon church. But it wasn't working out. The sky-soaring ecstasy he'd sought, the blinding flash that illumines the soul so that, in one instant, one sees all and knows all, as if the Green Flash, quite apart from its rare and wondrous beauty, were to grant him in the same instance, inner peace and wisdom; all this was denied him. He decided that his own ebullient spirit was inimical to life coenobitic[2]. Besides, he wanted to get laid.

So Apollo yielded to Dionysius, St. Paul to Baudelaire. Perhaps by drinking, wenching, and pursuing the profligate life he could, from the depths of the gutter, aspire to and even reach the stars. The road of excess led to the palace of wisdom.

---

[2] monastic

Chapter 3

Voyage to Fort Poontuk

"**O**h, I'm afraid there's no appeal from the decision of the D. Met and the board," explained Mr. Bodnar. "You'll be required to serve a year's time with Mr. Trent up at Fort Poontuk."

"But I won't be able to attend the University this fall," said Geoff, distraught, nervous and exhausted. "What happens to my bursary?"

Mr. Bodnar, who because he was left with but two front teeth looked startlingly rat-like, waved a pale hand.

"As I've explained before, Mr. Geoff, why don't you listen to me? Nothing happens to your bursary. It'll be waiting for you when you get back. Just resign yourself to the fact you've lost a year of University because of your...well... you know.."

"But what's going to happen to me! I have my studies, my books! And you're sending me off to some god-forsaken spot without books, without libraries, without culture." Geoff leaped from his chair and started pacing the room. "I don't believe this is happening to me. Like Candide! I've been found out in some minor peccadillo, and now I'm being thrown out of the country. Exiled by the Nazis!"

The wind whistled by Bodnar's two front teeth.

"What on earth are you talking about?" he asked.

"What I'm talking about is that I have a contribution to make to this dull as dishwater society we call Canada... we call Alberta. I have ideas, Bodnar, ideas to breathe a little life into this intellectual desert. Oh my God!"

"My dear Mr. Geoff, that may all be very well and good," said Mr. Bodnar. "But all we expect of you here is a good job done on the maps. A job which you haven't been doing to the best of your ability. Of course, you know we can't force you to go up north. You can always quit."

Geoff collapsed in the chair with a sigh. "I bow to Mammon," he said.

That very day Geoff swore an oath to continence and chastity. He held his flaccid penis in his hand and regarded it with loathing and contempt. The sceptre and found of man's greatness and despair, he thought, and for me it's meant nothing but trouble. He had a willy-nilly idea pop into his head. Was it Freud who had pointed out that sexual energy was so inexhaustible that if diverted toward creative things it produced genius? It's true, thought Geoff. The great ones, the Leonardos, Beethovens, Newtons, they don't get married, they don't fool with women. They used this instinctual powerhouse to rise above their fellow creatures, who are trapped as surely as rats in a cage, by their sexual instincts. Conversely, the perversion of the sexual instinct produces that monstrosity of humankind, the sex pervert, capable of any outrage, such as digging up half-rotted corpses to appease a necrophilian bent. He remembered reading somewhere of a frustrated young sculptor. He'd wrapped a rubber band around his penis so tightly that the thing had practically rotted off, which was what the sculptor wanted! Get rid of the penis! Turn all that perniciously squandered energy into great works of art. If genius were the capacity to take infinite pains, then the sexual drive would provide infinite energy.

As if frightened by these contemplations, Geoff's penis bestirred itself. This action saddened him. It in no way communicated anything pleasant, and confirmed the penis's independent existence.

"Don't worry," said Geoff. "I won't be tying you up with rubber bands."

But he vowed to remain the penis's master and not the other way around.

It was a bright spring day when Geoff stepped onto the tarmac of the Edmonton Airport to board the twin-engine Dakota aircraft that would take him to Fort Poontuk. His normal euphoria was back and now Geoff found himself looking forward to the adventure. In his high good spirits he'd even rushed into Mr. Bodnar's office, wrung that man's hand and thanked him for the opportunity to visit Canada's North country.

"The land of the wendigo and the midnight sun!" he'd called it.

Now, stepping onto the plane, he fancied himself as one of those figures out of a Somerset Maugham story, leaving the home and hearth for some far-flung but vital post of Empire. He turned and waved and was rather startled to see some of the weather office people gathered on the rooftop to see him off. And was that Angela peeking from behind the theodolyte screen? He couldn't be sure, but his heart sang and he threw a kiss to all.

"Goodbye, au revoir, cheerio!" he shouted as the attendant shut the door.

There were a handful of passengers in the aircraft, which after the usual mysterious preliminaries, was airborne.
In a trice the city of Edmonton was gone and the rolling parkland beneath yielded quickly to scrub timber.

The plane put down at Fort McMurray, and several passengers got off. Then it was on to Fort Smith. More passengers alighted. Then came Fort Resolution, then Providence, and finally, Geoff became aware that he was the only passenger left. There was no stewardess. He sat alone. The plane droned on. A tiny thrill of fear, more a stimulus to his imagination really, roused Geoff when the thickening cloud deck below, having obscured the lakes and forest, now engulfed the plane itself. 'Ha! What have we here,' thought Geoff. Outside there was nothing to see, no point of reference to suggest motion. It was as though someone had covered the windows with white paint, completely sealing off the outside world. Now and then the aircraft's wing would emerge from the fog, beads of moisture trembling on its metal surface. Geoff indulged in a fancy: Somehow the airplane had skipped the world's time-space continuum and would be drifting in eternity forever.

Deprived of all stimuli, Geoff kept dozing off in spite of his efforts to stay awake. But he finally succumbed completely. He dreamed of a tall, lean figure in black against a huge, glaring cyclorama on a stage from the wings of which rolled great masses of cloud. As the cloud masses approached the lone figure, they solidified in some mysterious way and threatened to crush the life from the figure on stage. Then from the top and rear of the stage more masses came, became solid rock bearing down with irresistible force. Then a trumpet sounded; releasing silver notes that impinged on Geoff's ears with a startling familiarity. A lost chord, instantly recognized, then gone and forgotten again the instant the sound was lost. Then, all was flinders, sparks and confusion as the extraneous voice of the aircraft's captain crashed in upon the reverie: "Fort Poontuk in five minutes."

It was cold and snowing when they landed. Hard, brittle, grey flakes were falling, like chips from the dark and glowering sky. As the plane taxied in, Geoff could see a big, parka-clad man, his glasses glinting, and hearing-aid cord extending from the dark recesses of the hood, standing before a motley crowd of whites and Indians, all of them similarly dressed and all stamping the ground and flinging their arms about to keep warm. The motors stopped, and the door opened.

A tall man, with a handsome though fleshy face, and wearing the khaki-colored parka that smacked of government design, strode forward.

"Well", said Cy Trent. "You're the only one aboard, so you must be Jerome Geoff. Welcome to Fort Poontuk."

Trent introduced the newcomer to some of the others gathered for the arrival of the airplane. Two I.C. (the second in command) of the Signals Corps establishment, Sergeant Andy Sitter was there, as were Signalmen Appleyard and Parnell. Their remarks were perfunctory, as they were far more interested in the plane's cargo.

After the initial greetings, Trent was silent and watched what went on about him with indifference.

Geoff said: "Mr. Trent, I'm very interested in katabatic phenomenon. I'm from southern Alberta, and we get a lot of that sort of thing there. The Chinook wind, I mean."

"Ah, yes."

"Well, the weather was beautiful when I left Edmonton this morning, ceiling and visibility unlimited. But the plane was socked in since Fort Providence."

"Yes," said Trent.

Parnell had received four bottles of Irish whiskey. "Greatest stuff in the world!" he cried.

"Hasn't got the character of Scotch" said Geoff, leaving Trent to join the others.

"What the hell you talking about?" Parnell asked. His expression asked a second question: "Who's this nut?"

"Well, Scotch and Irish whiskies are made in the same way," said Geoff, all smiles. "Same ingredients, same recipe. However, in Scotland, the mash is cooked with a very pungent peat whose smoke gets into the mash and stays there. That's why Scotch has that distinctive smoky taste."

"Well, I never knew that," said Parnell, sarcastic. "Hey, you ever been to Scotland?"

"No, but my Uncle.."

"Then what the fuck you know about it, eh?"

Geoff smiled. "Ah, none of us here ever knew Plato, or Socrates, or Buddha or Christ, but we learn about these men in books. That's how I found out about Scotch and Irish whiskies." But Parnell had turned away and left Geoff standing alone.

It was a thirteen-mile trip from the airport to the Fort; a

bone-jarring trip over frost boils, pot-holes, corduroy log paving and steep-sided streams that threatened to capsize the jeep in every instance. The black brooding presence of the forest pressed in on either side and the visible world was contained within the swirling snowflakes within range of the lights.

The dark and cold and the snow were all in depressing contrast to the bright, spring-like weather that favored Geoff's departure from Edmonton. During a lull in the conversation - - and it was dull stuff about spring break-up, and somebody named, Salt - - Geoff broke in: "I look upon this trip as an opportunity to do some heavy reading. It isn't everybody who gets a chance like we have. So, I'll be reading 'War and Peace, 'Don Quixote" and 'The Golden Bough"."

"Oh, goody-goody gum-drops!" said Parnell, fed up. "We'll see how long you stick with your books once Hannah-Maria gets swishing her tail around the place."

"Well, you oughta know all about Hannah-Maria, Parnell. When are you and your buddy Crunk gonna get together for another big orgy?" Appleyard said, laughing at Parnell's obvious discomfort.

Sergeant Andy Sitter, his moon face glowing, joined in: "Yeh, Parnell, but I hear the Bishop himself consecrated the proceedins." Sitter was using a comic Irish accent. "And I hear that the blessed Saints themselves came down from heaven to watch, and seein what was going on were after joinin' in the blessed sacrements themselves."

"That's blasphemous, Andy" snapped Parnell. "You shouldn't go around making comments like that."

But Appleyard was not through: "Well, faith and begorra!" he said.

"Ah, shut up, all of you" said Parnell. "'Sides, we shouldn't be talking like this. What's the kid gonna think about this town?"

"Hannah-Maria," said Geoff. "What an awful name."

A howl went up from the previous speakers.

"Well," said Sitter, "like the man said, 'a rose by any other name would smell as sweet'."

Trent spoke: "I wouldn't worry abut Hannah-Maria if I were you, Jerry. She's probably dosed up to the eyebrows and crawlin' with crabs."

Appleyard was to celebrate his fifteenth wedding anniversary next Wednesday, and had bought a full case of whiskey for that occasion. A bottle of it had been consumed by the time the jeep reached the single men's quarters.

The snow was coming down heavier, but this didn't deter Scotty, the cook, who rushed out and stood with a fixed anticipatory smile while his liquor was located. Then, Sitter took the jeep to make the other deliveries around town.

Geoff was shown his room, one of three located on the corners of the main recreation hall. The kitchen and main entrance to the quarters occupied the fourth corner, whose windows gave out onto the road and the riverbank, which could be viewed intermittently in the swirling snow. The place was equipped with a flush toilet and electric lights. In case of failure of the former, Scotty showed Geoff a detached wooden toilet seat, permanently installed behind the stove to keep it warm. The seat fitted the hole in the outhouse.

"It's back to the life of an Anchorite[3] for me!" enthused Geoff, who was delighted with his room. The furnishings consisted of a bed, a desk, a gooseneck lamp, chair, and a plywood wardrobe. Through the window over the bed, he could see the Station and the Stevenson screen, which housed the thermometers.

Scotty cooked a dinner of ham and eggs for Geoff, apologizing because he had to prepare the sideboard for the party which would inevitably take place.

"Y'know," he began. "It's never planned. It just

_____

[3] Religious hermit.

happens. And if I did'na have the stuff here, they'd be... well, they would'na know what to do."

Scotty had been nipping on his bottle all evening and, having completed his work, went to his accustomed chair, sat down, and fell asleep.

The guests began to arrive. First, signalman Warrant Officer, Michael Bonnycastle, who, over the most ritualistic protestations of his wife, started the punchbowl with a quart of over proof rum. Within an hour, most of the white population of Fort Poontuk, eager to meet the new man, had jammed into the room. The signalmen in their uniforms, and their wives, even Dr. Fleming dropped in to be introduced. Henpecked Patrice Prout, the HBC factor, stole in, shook Geoff's hand, bolted a drink, and stole back out again. Constable Ken Button of the R.C.M.P. was there and for a time he chatted with everybody, including May Dunn, the town's bootlegger. Likely as not, Button would be obliged to fine May three hundred dollars next month. This usually happened every June. People made jokes about it; said it was on the standing orders of the Fort Poontuk RCMP outpost: 'Every June fine May Dunn three hundred dollars'. May lived with Harry Crum, who stood around morosely, sipping on a glass of powdered milk to ease his raging heartburn.

"Oh, I'm looking forward to my stay in Fort Poontuk," said, Geoff, his brown eyes flashing. His cheeks were flushed. "It'll afford me an opportunity to really find out what life's all about."

His audience stared at him unsure quite how to respond.

"What I mean," he continued, "is that I may be able to find the True Way."

"Oh, you're religious like," said Helen Appleyard. She hadn't finished her first drink.

"Well, not exactly," explained Geoff. "You see, there are two ways of breaking through life's restrictions of flesh, time and space. By denying oneself, by the Apollonian way, mortification of the flesh, starvation, shutting oneself away from all distractions, like the plains Indians used to do..."

"No screwing around, eh?" asked Helen Appleyard.

"No! Nothing like that," responded Geoff. "By complete denial of the flesh and its appetites, one might reach the Enlightenment. Nirvana! But there are other ways to free the soul. Have you ever heard the saying, 'The road of excess leads to the palace of wisdom?'"

"Oh, I'm sorry," said Iris Bonnycastle. "I'm afraid I wasn't listening for a moment. Excuse me, there's my husband over there. Oh, Mickey! Fetch me another drink? Oh, never mind, I'll get it myself."

The Trents arrived.

"I could murder my husband," Jean Trent said to Geoff following the introduction. "I wanted him to bring you to our place for dinner. I'll bet all you got here was ham and eggs." She smiled at him. "But you seem to be doing all right."

Elsewhere in the room, Constable Button was talking with some of the signalmen and May Dunn.

"Well, I can't check on all these things, you know," he said. But as far as I know, Hannah-Maria isn't pregnant. Hasn't even got herself a new boyfriend yet so far as I know."

"You men," said May Dunn. "Here's a perfectly beautiful girl that's going to lose her looks and her figure - - and wow! What a figure, gotta admit I admire it myself -- just because you men can't keep your hands off her. Sure she's got two kids. But she's looking after them! But where are the fathers, eh? I'll tell you, the buggers are over the hills and far away."

Parnell and Nichol emitted sickly laughs.

"Yeah, it's true," Button was scratching his head. "But I tell you what. Next time... next time, we're going to have to find the father. I don't know exactly what we'll do, mind you. Maybe the crown will have to lay the paternity suit, but the

Government's getting sick and tired of footing all the bills for somebody else's fun."

Those around Button laughed. Parnell and Nichol headed for the punchbowl.

And so the party wore on, getting louder by the minute. Nor was the talking diminished when Joe Caribou and his Caribou Rats arrived tuned up and started to play. They were three: Joe, who played the violin and two guitarists, his cousins. They came marching in like condemned men, their heads hung low, neither smiling nor deigning to remove their heavy parkas and mukluks. They positioned themselves at one end of the hall, and Joe looked over the crowd. He, when he chose to speak, ruefully boasted of being the ugliest man in the Northwest Territories. Indeed, his face was cruelly scarred by smallpox and his nose was askew. But he played the violin with an astonishing virtuosity; there were no teachers of the instrument in Poontuk. His accompanists, two very much younger men, seemed destined to match his musical skills. So they stood, stolid and unsmiling, playing a repertory that ranged from "Squaws along the Yukon" to "My Home on the Fraser".

The attendees quickly became drunk. There was never any beer or wine at these affairs, and, try as they might, no one seemed to adjust to the potency of over proof rum. People found it necessary to shout in conversation, because of the exuberance of others. The area around the punchbowl became slippery with dripping and spilt drinks, and many skidded or fell, always getting a laugh from the others.

Trent was miserable. He came to the parties, had one or two drinks, and then wanted to go home. He was completely out of his element with these men and women, and privately to his wife, Jean, had branded them boors. But Jean was friendlier, more adaptable than her husband. If the parties were not exactly fun they were at least a respite from

Fort Poontuk's everyday boredom. The others liked her and followed her lead as she called for spot dances, polkas, or square dances. She told Trent that the difference between him and her was that he had come from old blue-law Toronto, while she was a child of far more easygoing southern Saskatchewan.

"That may be so," said Trent, as he waltzed clumsily to Joe Caribou's ponderous rendition of: "When the Ice Worms Nest Again". "But frankly, I wouldn't be here at all if it weren't for the material I need on the Katabatic winds."

"Oh, I know" she said. "But you'll get it done, Cy. You'll win out over this adversity. What was that motto you had in the Air Force, 'per Ardua ad Astra', that's right: 'Through Adversity to the Skies'. You'll make it and make me very proud of you when they start calling you Doctor Trent. But you'll always be my guy, Cy."

She was a little tight.

Trent usually insisted on going home with the arrival of Paul Salt, whom he couldn't stand. He had made an effort to like him, but Salt was an ignorant, monosyllabic asshole as far as Trent was concerned. A dangerous man, too, with definite manic tendencies, else why did he shut himself up in his room for days at a time, compulsively working on a Heath-Kit radio that never seemed to get finished. Salt, Trent noticed, was a sullen, silent drinker, whose infrequent remarks were always nasty, personal and taunting. Trent had no use for this small, dark man with his blue jowls.

Salt had finished his shift at the station, and with sergeant Sitter, Nichols and Appleyard, was having a drink. They'd been talking about hunting and fishing, and Salt regaled them with a story of his own. Salt had trapped frogs back home in Winnipeg, and had rammed lighted fire-crackers into their mouths. Then he'd toss the frogs into the air and watch them explode. "Boy, there was guts all over the place!"

"Come along, Jean," said Trent. "We're going home."

"Oh, Cy, no! Just one more dance and then we'll go."

"Jean," Trent's voice took on an edge. "Now."

"Watsamatter, Trent?" said Salt, leaning against the doorway into the kitchen and looking up at Trent through eyes half-closed to shut out the smoke of the cigarette dangling from his lips. "Why don't ya stay like the little lady says. Whatsa matter, don't ya like it here?"

Trent felt his gorge rising. What was the mater with him? His first impulse was to tell Salt to go to hell, but for some reason, he couldn't do this.

Salt smiled crookedly. "How come," he asked. "How come you always bog off when I come to the party? Eh, how's that?"

Again, Trent said nothing. He was confused and undone at the strength of his feelings against the smaller man, and at the seeming apathy of those about him, who didn't seem to appreciate the man's stupidity and vulgarity.

"He's coming home because I want him in bed," said Jean, laughing and tossing her head. "And you, miserable little runt, can go on blowing up frogs till you look like one."
Everyone laughed

"You didn't have to make any comments like that," snapped Trent when they'd walked outside. "I could handle that little black bastard."

"No, you couldn't, Cy" she said, taking her husband by the shoulders. "Life in this little town can be awfully tough. Particularly on a guy like you. You're not a soldier, or a hewer of wood or a drawer of water. You're a scholar, all by yourself with nobody to talk to, and I think it's upsetting you. You could squish that little Salt character under your thumb if you had to. Salt is like an insect that gets under your hide. Don't let him do it!"

"Yeah, well, how can I face up to him if you're jumping in all the time? You'll have to let me fight my own battles. Listen to me! Listen to what I'm saying. You're not my big brother, or my father, you're my wife, and I have to tell you not to fight my battles."

"It won't happen again, I promise" said Jean, smiling in the strange twilight of the north country, a twilight that would not yield to the night. "Now that you have your assistant, you have somebody to talk shop with and work with, and we'll both get out of here quicker."

Trent smiled. Softly, he said: "As usual, Jean, you're right. It's going to be better for us now."

"Of course it will," affirmed Jean. "But Cy, for heaven's sake, don't get so wrought up about things. It'll all work out okay. C'mon, let's get home."

They walked. Around them the dogs howled and snarled and rattled their chains. Cabins here and there shook with shouts, laughter and singing.

Some of the signalmen were gathered in the kitchen. In the common room the wives gathered about the newcomer, whose non-stop dialogue was punctuated now and then by raucous laughter and some question, posed in a high, giggly falsetto by one of the women: "But Hierogious... or whatever your name is...d'you really think you can screw your way into heaven?" The answer drowned in shrieks of laughter.

"Gotta do something," muttered Appleyard. He was staring at the floor and weaving with his back to the stove. "Can't have a fiasco like we did last year. That was awful." Nichol, ever the peacemaker, said: "That's right. We gotta do something different."

"Well, I got an idea." Parnell winked knowingly. He had the solution to the problem up his sleeve and was now about to reveal it. "Now listen. I don't care who it is, but somebody has got to get right out in the middle of the river this time, and put the stake down there. I'm telling you, right in the middle of the river. You don't do that, it'll never work."

"You know, you're right, Pat!" said Nichol. "A stake in

the middle, like through Dracula's heart, that's what we need."

"Won't work," said Appleyard, still looking at the floor. "Who the hell would be dumb enough to go out in the middle of that river and drive in a stake. It's just about to go, right now! You gotta be crazy!"

"You've got a good point there, Appleyard" said Nichol.

"Bullshit!" cried Parnell. "Look what happened on the river sweepstakes last year. Just a goddamn fuck-up! 'Cause the ice broke up in the middle first and the stake was in near the riverbank for Chrissake and didn't move and didn't set off the fire alarm for days after."

"Well, I can certainly see you've a valid argument," said Nichol, taking another drink.

"All right, all right! But I tell you what! Let's go back to the old way," said Appleyard. "To hell with tying it on to the siren. We have a man at the station all day and night. Let's leave it up to him. Let him put down the time when the ice first starts to move. Then there won't be any argument about the Goddamn stake and the siren."

"That sounds like a pretty good suggestion to me," said Nichol.

"Oh, yea, who says?" snapped Parnell. "And what happens if you have a ticket for four o'clock in the morning and the river goes out at five..or three, eh? You could always say the river went out at four instead of three or five, eh, and nobody would know the difference."

"Are you trying to call me a liar," demanded Appleyard. "By, golly, you know, Pat's got a pretty good point there, " said Nichol.

"No, No!" interjected Parnell. "I'm not calling you a liar, for Chrissake. I'm just trying to show you what would happen." Parnell lowered his voice: "Maybe somebody like that little fart-ass, Salt."

Nichol rolled his eyes. "Yeh, Salt" he said. "He just

might be the kind of guy."

"Gotta do something," muttered Appleyard.

There was trouble in the common room. A glass crashed to the floor, chairs scraped, women screamed. A loud, angry voice, spewing a string of obscenities, quashed the hubbub of the party.

The men dashed from the kitchen.

"It's that bloody Salt again!"

"Where's Button?"

"Went home hours ago", came the response.

Salt, drunk and staggering, his eyes blazing, was weaving in front of the group. Salt flung his arm in the general direction of his bedroom.

"I live in this place," Salt said drunkenly. "It's my home here. I don't want you in here, you rotten cock..."

Geoff, obliviously happy and smiling, came forward. "Now, now, now!" Geoff said. "Let's have none of that! Let's all get along together!"

Smack! Salt had spun around, and more by accident than design, had caught Geoff on the cheek with his open hand and sent him thudding into the wall.

Bonnycastle, who'd been watching the fracas with bleary amusement and hoping it would blow over, now took command.

"Salt!" he barked. "This has gone far enough. Any more trouble with you and it'll cost you a month's trade pay. Go to your room!" And, unable to control himself, Bonnycastle turned quickly away.

For a moment Salt stood his ground, looking at those around him, his face torn by hatred and sorrow. He closed his eyes and bowed his head slightly. "Everybody, I'm sorry," Salt said slowly, turned and went to his room.

His door had no sooner closed than the hubbub resumed.

Geoff, none the worse for his encounter, was up on his

feet and looking out the window. He was marveling at the fact that, though it was two o'clock in the morning, the sun was cruising the eastern horizon. He went outside for a better look, and while standing on the road, came close to being knocked down by a swiftly passing dog-team.

The party was breaking up now. The women were putting on ski pants, which they wore under their skirts coming to and from the parties. All shrugged into heavy parkas and left, guiding their way by flashlight. In the steely cold air, the mukluks crunched loudly in the new-fallen snow as the men and women, bundled up like bears, made their way home.

Chapter 4

Trent's Crusade

It had happened before the war. A clerk at the Hudson's Bay Post at Poontuk, who had complained about the twenty below zero weather at seven o'clock in the morning, had gone outside at noon to find water dripping from the roof. A mild, gentle wind, blowing in from the Mackenzie Mountains to the west had wrought the astonishing change in the weather.

It was the north's first recorded instance of a species of wind celebrated the world over, with names like Harmattan, Sirocco, Mistral, Williwaw, Waff, Zonda, Willy-Nilly, and Chinook. They are not an unmixed blessing. The French Mistral drives men to rape and murder, and police reinforcements are sent in, as a matter of practice whenever the Mistral starts to blow. The wind was blowing when Van Gogh cut off his ear, and when he took his own life. It is a wind that sends the incidence of mental depression soaring when the Fohn blows at Munich, or the Chinook, in Calgary. The Sirocco in North Africa regularly sends the temperature soaring above one hundred and thirty degrees Fahrenheit.

Nothing quite as spectacular as that had occurred at Fort Poontuck, nor was it likely to. The wind didn't occur that often, and so far as Trent was concerned, this was to his advantage, allowing him to fix on those atmospheric phenomena that were extent when the warm wind occurred, with plenty of control data from Poontuk's usual, unrelenting cold. The change from cold to warm at Poontuk, when its wind did occur, was perhaps the most pronounced in the world. At least Trent was at Poontuk to find out.

As a meteorologist, he was also expected to make forecasts, based on local observations and experience.

Officially, all the forecasting for the northern part of the country came from Edmonton, which drew weather reports from across the north, indeed for all over the world. Weather reports from the northernmost weather station at Alert Bay on Ellesmere Island and throughout the western Arctic were funneled through Fort Poontuk. These reports kept coming on a twenty-four hour basis, where they were collated and transmitted by radio to Edmonton. Trent used this material in his own forecasting and had, on more than one occasion, issued a forecast at variance with the official one from Edmonton. Trent's weather map showed a storm passing to the south, across southern British Columbia and Alberta, and while the weather might get colder, a flight from Poontuk to Yellowknife could be made with clear skies and helpful tail winds. Trent's performance on this occasion did not escape the attention of the Edmonton newspapers, who bannered stories about a "mystery forecaster in the frozen north, who foretells weather with uncanny accuracy." The same articles demanded to know why this meteorological marvel was languishing in the North country and not permitted to exercise his genius for the greater weal in Edmonton. This situation was decried as still another example of typical governmental bungling.

Meantime, Trent had wanted to do more analysis of the upper atmosphere over Poontuk in connection with his studies. This required hydrogen for balloons, a theodolite to follow the balloons, and eventually, since observations the year-round, and on a regular basis were deemed necessary, the construction of a special building to house hydrogen generating equipment. Nepomuk Permaneder, Trent's carpenter, was scheduled to finish that job this summer.

Nepomuk Permaneder, who had flown into Poontuk a few weeks prior to Geoff's arrival, had, when asked if he had a cramped leg from the trip, informed them in a heavy German accent that he had a wooden leg. He slapped it heartily and told Trent and the others that he'd lost it during the First World War while fighting with the German army, and in an engagement in which he'd been awarded the Iron Cross, Second Class. Nepomuk Permaneder didn't make any bones about it.

He noticed the military medal decoration on Appleyard's uniform and said, "Vot de Hell, zo I vas in der Cherman Army and yo's in der Canadian. So vot? So us poor bastards vere all in der zame boat togetter and who gifs a damn on whose side vich?" Then, he had whipped out a bottle of scotch from his back pocket and proffered drinks all around.

"You'll do all right in this town," Trent had said.

The arrival of Jerome Geoff now gave Trent more of an establishment than he had ever anticipated. He began to think about a radio-sonde station at Poontuk: This would require much larger balloons to carry aloft instrument packages that would transmit information of temperature, pressure and other meteors up to tremendous heights. But that could wait. Trent was satisfied for the present with his work and a special weather office that had been built onto the Signal Corps radio station for his personal use. He would call his paper: "Katabatic and Fohn Wind Phenomenon on the Upper Mackenzie Valley".

These esoteric studies intrigued Appleyard.

"Trent," he said. "Just what the hell do you do in here all day?"

Trent was happy to explain, and at length, about his correlating the upper winds with surface temperatures, and the movement of low and high pressure systems across the north. Seeking to find that rare combination of "meteors", as Trent called atmospheric phenomenon, that would create the warm winds in the upper Mackenzie. Appleyard was surprised at all this. He'd never seen Trent show such enthusiasm. Trent invited Appleyard to look over pages and pages of mathematical notations, as he kept up a steady stream of talk about isobars, entropy, albedo, and super-saturated adiabatic lapse-rates.

Trent was beginning to wonder when the warm wind phenomenon would occur. He'd been in the North two winters, and while there'd been plenty of signs to indicate the wind might occur, these signs had failed. Trent found himself with a growing mass of interlocking statistical data, "meteorological marginalia" he called it, over which he lucrubrated[4], seeking the elusive clue to solve the mystery. He spent more and more time at his desk, badgered the Edmonton meteorological office for special papers and information, and demanded more weather reports and observations of the signalmen. These men wondered about Trent, wondered what he found so overpoweringly interesting in pouring over endless reams of figures, when he had a good-looking wife waiting at home.

If the signalmen had harbored notions that eccentricity of character was prerequisite in a weatherman, these notions were confirmed with the arrival of Trent's assistant, who styled himself Heironymous Geoff after a great painter. No sooner had this zany person arrived, (and started running off at the mouth) than he set up an easel on the road outside the single men's quarters and started painting. Geoff said he wanted to capture the elusive moment poised between winter and spring in the North country. Geoff babbled on about Tom Thomson, Van Gogh, impressionism, or who knew what. Geoff also had a typewriter at which he pecked far into the night. So here were the pair of them: Trent pouring over his weather reports and statistics, and Heironymous Geoff painting and typing. No wonder weather forecasts were often wrong!

Bonnycastle exploited Geoff's typing skills to the advantage of his station and the community in general. He

---

[4] Night study, especially written meditations.

had Geoff prepare a news report, which was included in a monthly news-sheet, "Notes of Interest" printed in Edmonton and circulated among the Signal Corps stations north of the sixtieth parallel. It wasn't long before Fort Poontuk, which had not contributed much of note before, was commanding more space in "Notes of Interest" than even Fort Smith, the territory's provisional capital. The harried editor was after Bonnycastle to have his correspondence cut down.

Since Geoff always assumed that his personal history was of consummate interest to everybody, it was soon known to all that he had been orphaned at a very early age. For the Signalmen, that followed a pattern. The only one of their number queer enough to qualify for membership in the looney weatherman's club would be Paul Salt. He was an orphan too, and the only home he had ever really known was the army.

Chapter 5

Paul Salt and Jean Trent

It was one of those parties when everybody was getting too drunk too fast, and the whole thing was bound to end up in calamity. The supply plane had flown in with a full quart of pure grain alcohol for the punch-bowl and in no time the party reached the stage normally arrived at by three o'clock in the morning. The men were on one side of the room singing: "That was a Cute Little Rhyme". While the lyrics started off, reasonably smutty:

"There was a young man from Boston,

Who owned a baby Austin,

He had room for his ass,

And a gallon of gas,

But his balls hung out and he lost 'em"

. . . they tended to deteriorate, as, the verse being passed from one person to another, each singer tried to "top" the other using shock and bombast.

"There was an old whore from Tours,

Whose ass was all covered with sores,

As she walked down the street,

The dogs snapped at the meat,

That hung in green gobs from her drawers"

"Now, that's gone far enough!" shouted Jean Trent, who came forward and mockingly shook Parnell's hand. "My congratulations to you, Sir, on coming up with the filthiest piece of the entire evening." She signaled to the party for a round of applause while Parnell beamed.

"But," she continued. "It's time for a little something in which the girls can join in as well. What do you say, girls?"

"Yaaaa!" bawled the assembled women.

It was then that Jean introduced them to the parlor game of charades. About which, to her astonishment, none of the others knew anything. First attempters at the game generated more fun than among more practiced players and persons who normally took little or no part were drawn in almost in spite of themselves. Paul Salt, for one, found himself laughing almost to tears at some of the antics. Sergeant Sitter, looking more than ever the big fat Dutchman, trying to act out "Snow White and the Seven Dwarfs" was the best.

Jean was at the party alone. Cy Trent was busy at the weather office. Jean had turned her brown eyes toward Salt, and, seeing him alone, had smiled. Salt felt a strange combination of shyness and anticipation. The feeling might have passed, but then she came forward, and taking him by the arm, said: "C'mon, Paul, you and I will show these donkeys what it's all about."

He got a faint whiff of her perfume. It was fresh and flowery. He felt her warmth and softness as she took him into the kitchen. He was surprised, delighted and a little breathless as she enthusiastically explained the way she'd planned to act out her charade. They would sit on the floor, making rowing motions in unison and pausing to burp every third stroke. "Our side will be sure to get 'The Vulgar Boatman'-- get it?" she burped. "I saw it done in a movie years ago, maybe they've seen it, too."

"Oh, I dunno..." said Salt. Suddenly, he felt apprehensive, as if he might blush.

"Oh, no you don't" said Jean. "Don't let me down now, Paul." And with that she pushed him out into the common room, hitched up her skirt, and sat on the floor.

She and Paul did their stunt, but failed to communicate the answer to their side. The revelation of what they'd been about brought a round of applause and laughter from everyone. Jean kissed Paul on the cheek, and told him he owed her a drink. Salt's heart was singing as he dashed to the bar.

Trent had come in looking pale and grim. Salt had seen

him having words with Jean, had seen that beautiful smile alter first to an expression of puzzlement, and then annoyance. Salt, at that time, had had a terrible urge to fling the drink in Trent's face. Jean's eyes caught his as he approached; they told him to never mind about the drink. Soon the Trents left, and Salt spent the evening in morose withdrawal as the party ebbed and flowed around him.

So, from one happy moment with Jean, Salt was more quickly knocked down into the dumps. After that incident, Jean no longer seemed so friendly, as if she'd been warned away from him. She might smile at him, but seemed reluctant to show anything more. Then, one evening, Salt watched Jean (he could hardly summon the determination ever to take his eyes off her) as she and her husband danced closer than usual, saw her mouth open as she raised her face to be kissed. Salt was assailed by feelings that almost overcame him; he was wide-eyed and shocked by the intensity of the force that suddenly welled up within him. Before he was aware of it, he had flung his glass to the floor, smashing it to smithereens, and unmindful of the calls and comments of the others, stomped out into the chilly night.

There, he had paced up and down, a solitary black figure on the snow-covered moonlight drenched scene, his breath gushing from his nostrils. His mind, as if prodding him with a torture instrument, returned again and again to the scene: Jean's mouth slowly opening to receive Trent's kiss, her eyelids sliding down, her body pressing closer. He tried to dash the vignette form his mind, but it redounded, a paroxysm that sickened and frightened him.

Some time later Salt, for thinking about Jean, found himself unable to sleep. He got up, dressed in parka and boots, and went outside. It was a clear, cold night. The stars glittered like myriad, merciless eyes, piercing through the dead-calm air, and the snow crunched as he walked. Then, he spied a light at Trent's house, and, using every precaution, he stole up and peeped through a chink in the lower part of the window. He could see nothing. Stealthily, he prowled around the house until he came to the bedroom. There was a small light over the vanity dresser, and seated there was Jean Trent! He stared as she fussed with her face, and then she stood up. She was wearing only underclothes and a slip, which she passed over her head. Salt's mittened hands flew to his face, covering his eyes. Without further thought he turned around and ran down the road, back to the single men's quarters, as fast as he could.

He was panting, sweating and in mental turmoil when he flung himself down onto his bed. It was some minutes before his composure returned, before that maddening scene of Jean with her open mouth mercifully subsided. Now, he was filled with self-loathing. What was the mater with him? What made him go sneaking around, looking into people's windows? Early in the morning, he fell into a troubled sleep.

Chapter 6

The River Breaks Up

It was said that a Governor of the Hudson's Bay
Company, feeling tired and cramped after a long day's
canoeing, ordered a halt at the spot that was to become
Fort Poontuk. So it was here by chance; like a benign
wart on the northward pointing finger of the Mackenzie river,
and while for a time the wart showed some spontaneous
remission, it reversed itself and grew again during the war.
That was when tons of material and hundreds of soldiers,
airmen, and even sailors passed through during construction
of the Alaska Highway to the West. War's profligacy had left
a brand-new liberator bomber moldering on the airstrip, and
in the middle of the town, track-deep in the slowly devouring
permafrost, was a perfectly good Caterpillar tractor. Further
North along the river at Fort Norman there were more
leftovers of the conflict and these provide a curious story. A
dozen army trucks, brand new with practically no mileage,
had been left standing neatly in a row. A year after the war
they were still there. Nobody claimed them. It was then that
Frank and George appeared on the scene. They hired a
barge from the Northern Transportation Company and
drove the trucks onto it. The long-range plan was to ship the
trucks to Edmonton and sell them. But as the trip upstream
went along, alarm was raised. Various government agencies
along the route reported to higher authorities, which in turn
reported to Ottawa. What happened after that nobody knew,
except that signalmen at Poontuk were aware of messages
flying helter-skelter across the country as the barge moved
out of the Mackenzie onto Great Slave Lake. There, the
cargo was seized by mounted police and dumped overboard.
That was the end of the affair.

Frank and George, who together had survived the

hungry thirties, returned to Fort Poontuk, flabbergasted again at the mysterious ways of government.

The Fort settled down after the war to its normal somnolence. It was the last week in May.

"Goddamn spring break-up's late this year, George," said Frank.

The pair of them were hunkered down looking over the river.

"You damned ol' fool," retorted George. "It's been too cold, that's why. Can't expect it to thaw out until you get two or three good weeks of solid sunshine. Hey! Now what's going on here?"

Appleyard and Parnell were setting up a pole on the riverbank. They explained they would drive a long spike, about five feet long, into the river ice some distance out, then run a line from the spike over the pole, and attach the line to the fire siren. Tickets were already being sold on the break-up sweepstakes. Anyone with five dollars could get in on the gamble, on a winner-take-all basis, minus a few expenses.

The two signalmen were now discussing which one of them would take the spike out onto the river.

"Wouldn't go out there if I was you," warned George. "Looks to me like she's ready to let go anytime."

"What do you say we flip a coin?" asked Parnell. "Loser goes out and drives in the stake."

"That's good enough for me, " said Appleyard, as he drew a coin from his pocket. "Here, you call it."

"Wait a minute," protested Parnell. "This is asinine. You're right. Maybe we should just let the guy on shift make a note of the time the ice goes out."

"Nothin' doing, Parnell," snapped Appleyard. He smiled ruefully and waved his hand. "This is all your idea, remember, and there's no turning back."

"What's going on?" It was Geoff.

They briefly explained what they had in mind and closed

their explanation by emphasizing that no matter what the official time, the winning time would be when the siren sounded.

Geoff became excited. He grinned at the two signalmen and reached for the spike. "Here," he said. "Give it to me. I'll do it."

"Oh, I dunno.." Appleyard started.

Parnell interrupted. "Never mind. If the kid wants to do it, let him do it. Here!"

Geoff took the spike and climbed down the bank to the frozen river.

"Easy, sonny," said George.

Geoff kicked a block of ice that was lying on the river's bank. It shattered into a thousand tinkling shards of ice shaped like candles.

George was alarmed. "Well now, Boy! I think you better come up."

"Relax! It's okay," said Geoff. That candling doesn't mean a thing.

Geoff moved out into the jumble of frozen blocks that made up the river's surface. The blocks were fused into the ice below. He scrabbled quickly, pulling more and more of the line, paid out by Parnell, who stood on shore. At times, Geoff disappeared altogether behind some larger hummock, only to reappear, wave and move further outward.

The activity at the river bank soon attracted a buzzing knot of spectators. Mr. Prout of the Hudson's Bay Post and his wife, the store clerk and some Indians gathered to watch.

"Well, I never," said Mrs. Prout. "Will you look at that? The man must be out of 'is mind." She remarked with her cockney accent. "'E'll be killed, 'e will. The ice is just abat ready to go. 'adn't 'e best be warned off?"

Bonnycastle came striding up. "What's he doing out there?"

"It's the new weather-guy," said Parnell. "He wanted to

go."

"You idiots," exploded Bonnycastle. "Appleyard, for God's sake, why didn't you stop him? You two should have more sense." Bonnycastle cupped his mouth and shouted: "Geoff, come back right now! Come back!"

Geoff, whose figure was now quite small on the surface of the frozen Mackenzie river, was seen to stop, turn around, and make a shift to drive the spike in the ice.

A sharp report bounded up from the river, reverberated through the settlement, and crashed into the forest beyond.

"Oh my God!" breathed Bonnycastle. "My God! My God!"

A rent had appeared in the river upstream from Geoff, and was accompanied by a series of sharp cracks, like rifle bullets, passing overhead. The breach spread alarmingly across the two miles' width of the river. Then there was a great up-thrust, as if a thousand miles of ice choked river, sensing liberation from winter's grip, suddenly flung all its strength into the breach. The river ice crumbled under the pressure.

At first, the main thrust seemed upstream, against the main flow of the river. But this quickly changed, and those ashore could but watch in stunned horror as, in a wild profligacy of strength, the river carried blocks of ice as big as houses; thrusting some up, crushing some down, sending them grinding and crunching, shattering against the riverbank. The whole river from bank to bank was a scene of titanic disorder with a thunderous roar like a thousand avalanches. Closer to Geoff the river's breakup came, erupting towards him, who ran in a panic over the jumbled surface. Stumbling and falling, moving again, disappearing and reappearing, at last he reached the bank. The legs of his trousers were torn from his wild effort. Appleyard jumped down the bank to help him. Moments later, those frozen blocks were charging the bank, threatening to spill over while the liberated river gushed and spumed in turmoil. With the rage of a mighty creature, too long entombed in cold and darkness, the river burst upward, flinging off the coffin lid. As if the sun and the advancing season had nothing to do with it, the river had said: "Now is the time!"

Flushed from his near-death experience, Geoff nevertheless shook off those who crowded about him. They were wishing to show, in some manner, the strange fealty owed to one who'd been snatched from the jaws of death literally before their eyes. But Geoff dashed into his quarters and returned with his easel and paint.

"I must capture this moment," he exulted. "This is the day when Time begins. This is the day when Life returns to the earth. This is the day that says..." Geoff gazed out at the terrible moving wreck on the river's surface. Intoxicated either by the scene or his own verbosity, he concluded: "This is the day when Love conquers the world. 'Omnia vincit amor'."

There was no getting through to him, so they eventually left him alone at his picture, which, like most of the numerous others he had started, was never to be finished. The time of the river's break-up was simply taken from Bonnycastle's wristwatch.

Chapter 7

Dining with the Prouts

One of the more predictable occurrences for the newly arrived in Fort Poontuk was an invitation to sup with the Prouts. It was a long-standing custom in the community, an extension of hospitality, which, so far as anyone knew, had never been reciprocated. Except for a few items (bootleg whiskey, French safes, blue ointment, dirty magazines and books) which were vended by May Dunn, practically all consumer goods in the Fort were for sale only at the Hudson's Bay Post. You couldn't buy a white shirt there. In this community, a white shirt would last a lifetime. The store's inventory was made up of heavy woolen items, shirts, underwear and trousers. Most of the heavy outer wear, the parkas, mukluks and mitts were made and purchased from the local natives, for whose use, the store had a variety of traps, ammunition, and firearms, along with Hawaiian shirts, armbands, and tweed caps. One day, soon after Geoff's arrival, an attractive little girl knocked on the door of the single men's quarters, and, after asking to see Mr. Geoff, had presented him with a carefully hand-written invitation to dine at the Prout's three days hence.

Geoff hadn't seen Patrice Prout since that first party. His first impression was confirmed.

"Come in, come in" said Prout, as he answered Geoff's knock.

Mr. Prout was nervous and flitted about the living room, calling on his two attractive young daughters to help the guest off with his things. Then he sat in his chair, staring around and squirming, and chuckling every now and then to nobody in particular. He seemed to be striving desperately for something to say, and didn't offer Geoff a drink.

In came Mrs. Prout. Her face, the flesh of which purled

44

around the nose, a fiery monadnock, was powdered to a chalk white, in contrast to the henna-rinsed hair, which sprung out like a sullied nimbus. She was dressed in a flowery print dress, and escorted by an entourage of five or six cats that mewed, leaped and scampered about her as she moved toward Geoff.

"'Ow nice of you to come," she said. Her face crinkled in a smile. "Sit down, won't you?"

If Mr. Prout had difficulty in making conversation, such restraints did not bother his spouse.

Her face grew grave. "What d'ya think about all these dirty, syphilitic Poles they're bringing into the country?" she asked of Geoff.

"I beg your pardon?"

She repeated the question, and when Mr. Prout made bold as to suggest that their guest was not interested in the question of immigration to Canada, she grew graver still. She lit up a cigarette and puffed furiously. "Oh, yes. It's all right for you to sit there an' not worry. You've got a job. But the day will come, mark my words, when those dirty, syphilitic Poles and all the other Bohunks will take over all the colonies." She glared at her husband. "You're soft. That's what's the matter with you."

All this time, she had kept her eyes on Geoff, to see his reaction to her harangue against her husband. It was curious. While she was scolding poor Prout, she was smiling and nodding occasionally to Geoff, who was stricken dumb by the performance.

"Oh yes," she continued, "'E don't see it. Because like I say, 'e's soft. Soft in da 'ead. Dat's wot 'e is."

From this premise, she proceeded to call into question her husband's qualifications as a helpmate, pointing out that the wall-papering, the installation of the linoleum, and a few other jobs about the place had been on her initiative, and "da sweat o' my brow! Because 'e won't lift 'is 'and to turn anyting. Oh yes! 'e says 'e 'as 'is work in the store. Work indeed! I know what 'e's doing. 'E's casting lascivious eyes over da likes of dat slut 'annah-Mariah, dat's wot, while I wok and slave, I do, wearin' me fingas to da bone."

She flung away her cigarette, and quickly stoked up another. One of the girls rushed to pick up the discarded butt. "Tank you, Dearie," said Mrs. Prout, extending her hand as if offering it to be kissed.

"Oi! You've probably noticed dese goils 'aven't you. Well, dey aren't mine. Not on your life. Dey are the issue of lustful sheets. Lustful sheets d'you 'ear! Between my 'usband and some filthy, disease-ridden native goil, 'oo prob'ly 'ad da crabs!"

And she went on to explain how poor Prout had lived alone at the Post for three years before her arrival from England. The two young girls represented a second family for the Prouts, the first having now grown up and making their own way in England. "And wot d'you tink about dat?" she asked. The cats had now formed a kind of "cordon sanitaire" around her.

"Mrs. Prout," said Geoff. "I should like very much to paint your picture. I do some painting, you know."

Mrs. Prout was enormously flattered. Mr. Prout, who'd sat through the entire proceedings with a stunned smile now seemed sensible to what was going on.

"Yes, you see, Mrs. Prout" continued Geoff. "I can paint you as one of the great ladies of Greek Mythology."

"Oooh! 'oo?" asked Mrs. Prout.

Geoff was about to answer, 'Medusa'. He thought better of it, then roused himself to talk. He felt sorry for poor Prout and would come to his rescue. He would take the conversation away from the termagant.

"You're concerned about the Poles," he said. "Have you ever considered the poor male butterfly?"

"Well, I dunno..."

"Consider the male butterfly, Mrs. Prout," continued Geoff. "The poor creature is without a mouth. He can't eat. Isn't supposed to. In fact, his one and only function on this earth is to fertilize the female. Then he's finished and done with. He is thrown aside like an old shoe."

"Well, I.." began Mrs. Prout.

"Ah wait!" interrupted Geoff. "Consider the black widow spider. Do you know that the consummation of fertility only comes about when the female devours her mate? It's a fact. And what about the praying mantis? There, the same thing occurs. And do you know further, Mrs. Prout, that in certain species of fish, the male is reduced to practically nothing. In the Lophiformes fish, which inhabits the abyss, the male attaches himself to the female. Gradually, through a strange but marvelous transformation, the male's body is fused with the female's. Their blood systems, everything fuses, and the poor male shrinks away, until all that's left of him is a pair of testicles. But that isn't all, Mrs. Prout, consider if you will, the honey bee..."

Geoff continued thus all through dinner and the after ceremonies, which Mrs. Prout took pains to dispense in short order.

In taking his leave, Geoff's hand was pumped by Prout, who said, "Thank you, my boy, and God bless you!"

Chapter 8

Arrival of the Supply Barges

Heironymous Geoff was trying to play his recorder. Attempting Bach's "Jesu, Joy of Man's Desiring" his total ignorance of the instrument and his own complete lack of musical ability produced nothing but shrill caterwauling. Even Salt came out of his room to find out what was going on, and Nepomuk Permaneder, coming in for lunch, owned it to be the most 'God awful' noise he'd ever heard. Scotty, the cook, thought that since the weather was turning milder, Geoff would be better off practicing outdoors, about a mile in the bush.

"Men," said Geoff. His eyes had that far-off look they'd had after the river break up. "I'm merely trying to exalt myself as a human being. All human beings should learn to play some musical instrument because this is what separates them from animals and places them just below the angels. Leonardo Da Vinci was of the opinion that painting was music one could see. Walter Pater, centuries later, said that music was the highest form of art. Do you know why? Because the material you use and the expression desired in a work of musical composition are one and the same. It's a perfect blend of ethos and pathos and at the same time completely non-representational, so that it will appeal to all people for all time. What Leonardo and Pater were getting at is that any other art that approaches music becomes a better form. Poetry is better than prose, and abstract art better than photography. Do you understand?"

Salt went back to his room. Permaneder and Scotty kept staring at him for a moment, exchanged glances, and left. Geoff was about to take up his instrument again when a strange sound swept over the Fort. It was the far-off but distinct blast of a ship's horn. Everybody in the Fort stopped what he was doing and listened. Another blast. And with that the town was drawn to the riverbank. People came running from the Hudson's Bay Post, the radio station, the cabins, the white houses of the government, Harry Crum's hotel, from everywhere to line the bank, point at and wave to the line of barges, now but an inconsequential dash on the grey-brown surface of the Mackenzie. It was a fine day, sunny, calm and warm and a spontaneous cheer rang up from those on shore as the barges, being pushed by the tug "Radium Mackenzie" at last hove to at the upstream end of the Fort where the slope was gentle, and permitted access to the river's edge. The vessel was pushing about 20 barges, arrayed in two files before it, and surmounting each barge was a huge tarpaulin, ten feet high, covering the cargo beneath.

For the weather office there were barrels of diesel fuel, caustic soda, aluminum for the hydrogen generator, wood and other material for the hydrogen shack. There was as well a year's supply of food for the Trents and Geoff with everything, from 100 pounds of dehydrated potatoes to a case of sweet biscuits itemized. The army's manifest was similar. And there was a piano for Canon Ford; and an outboard motor for Sergeant Sitter; a case of books for Trent and Geoff; furniture for the Parnells; a refrigerator for the Appleyards; big boxes, wrapped in plain brown paper for May Dunn and Harry Crum; a bicycle for the Prout kids... The natives went to work for the Army, the Department of Transport, the RCMP, and the Hudson's Bay Company, while Frank and George hired out their services and their truck. After the landing, preliminaries were few. The captain did not come ashore. In this there was some disappointment, but the community leaders were assured by the purser that there was no implied slur to Fort Poontuk, quite the contrary. At the last stop, the Captain, who represented Santa Claus, summer and all good things, bringing sweetness and light to the communities along the Mackenzie had been feted so well that he'd been incapacitated for two days, and was just now showing signs of renewed interest in life; but not so much as to risk another Northern reception.

Throughout the long June day, the work of unloading the barges went on, and was finished by nine o'clock. As there was still plenty of sunlight, a challenge was issued to the crew for a ball game. But the Captain, through an intermediary, let it be known he wouldn't release the crew, the flotilla would not linger in Poontuk. An hour later, the "Radium Mackenzie" and its barges had disappeared downstream. Nobody in Fort Poontuk wanted to call it a day. The sun, after a half-hearted dip toward the horizon, sprang back, and its refusal to comply with normal behavior was transmitted to the world below.

Further north, the Eskimos go temporarily insane with the return of the sun. The long Arctic night, with its strict and unrelenting pressure, suddenly was vanquished before the swelling glory of the sun. The human spirit burst forth like a flower. Eskimos actually changed color from brown to purple, their cheeks glowed red, their eyes glazed. For days, they would wander about, unable or unwilling to sleep, stunned by the ever-strengthening sunlight, and succumbing to sleep only when exhausted. Sometimes even in sleep the wandering continued, as if the implacable sun, denied the right to rest, were spitefully instituting the same regime among people. Tennyson's celebrated verse about spring and a young man's fancy most certainly held sway in these circumstances. There was copulation, continuously, inexhaustibly and insatiably anytime and anywhere, outside propriety and modesty. Perhaps with the encroachment of the white man this madness had disappeared, perhaps not. It was never quite so pronounced in the lower latitudes. But the more extreme example serves to illustrate the effect on those set free after being too long in cold and darkness pent.

Fort Poontuk received a visitor from the barges. He was Jack Mazooli, a photographer on assignment from MacLean's Magazine. Everybody was quickly apprised of this because he went about pumping hands and declaring: "Hi, I'm Jack Mazooli, on assignment from MacLean's Magazine." A small young man, Mazooli's slight form was festooned with cameras, light metres, leather lens cases and other esoteric paraphernalia, and he also carried a long wooden box prominently marked with the words: "Jack Mazooli, photo." He bore a letter from the Signal Corps Colonel in Edmonton requesting the hospitality and good offices of the Signal Corps Post at Poontuk.

Mazooli had no sooner set foot on land than he spotted Hannah-Maria.

He was lucky he'd reached Poontuk at the best time possible for the indulgence of his craft. People down north[5] are warmer than those in the southern latitudes. Because the latter throughout the winter months make few concessions to the weather, going about dressed in suits, shirts, and ties while women wear their skirts even though the temperature may be forty below. No such nonsense was countenanced down north. Here there was no compromising with the weather; everybody wore woolen underwear, heavy melton ski pants with storm cuffs, bulky woolen shirts; puffy, down-filled parkas with fur-fringed hoods, and seal-skin mukluks, so that everybody on a cold day waddled about like the young children of over-solicitous parents, innocent and androgynous. But with the warmer weather, winter's chrysalis fell away and sexual distinction returned. In

---

[5] "Down North was a popular expression for communities sited along the Mackenzie river. This is because the Mackenzie flows north from Great Slave Lake and empties into the Beaufort Sea on the Arctic Ocean. Since in 1947, most supplies had to be floated in to remote outposts by barges after spring break-up, the downstream, or north direction came to be referred to as "down north".

Hannah-Maria's case, this return was spectacular. Here she was in a skirt and sweater entirely too tight for her, an image of bulging breasts, high set buttocks and long naked legs growing from incongruous high-heeled shoes.

"Wow!" cried Jack Mazooli, rushing forward to let it be known that he was, "Jack Mazooli, on assignment from MacLean's Magazine."

In no time, Mazooli had brought the business of unloading the barges to a stand-still. At first, Hannah Maria blushed that she'd never had her picture taken before but was obviously impressed, and succumbed to Mazooli's blandishments.

"Now, put your hands behind your back. That's right! Take a deep breath, fill up that chest! Way to go! Now, bring those shoulders back. That's right. Look over your shoulder, right into the camera and smile. C'mon now, a nice, big smile! Wow! That's it!" cried Mazooli.

Some of the crewmen from the barges wanted to leave their work and have a closer look. The purser had to issue threats about loss of pay to keep them aboard. Bonnycastle suggested to Mazooli that there was more to be photographed in Poontuk than Hannah-Maria, and asked that he at least move along.

"Good idea!", agreed Mazooli, who left, taking Hannah-Maria with him.

During this while, Geoff had been attending to the weather office cargo and had persuaded Frank and George to let him drive their truck. This was agreeable to them, until, coming up over the hill, Geoff's glance caught sight of the raven-haired Hanna-Maria. Her big, white, teeth were exposed in a shameless grin as she hiked her skirt over her thighs. Mazooli was shouting, and engrossed in these sights and sounds, Geoff's attention wavered. The truck veered toward the riverbank.

"Jesus Christ, Kid!" bellowed George, reaching and

wrestling control of the steering wheel. "What you're trying to kill us all!"

"My God," breathed Geoff, "it's a lucus natura." His eyes still fixed on the girl.

"Don' know about that," said Frank. "But she's a Goddamn good piece of tail, so I hear!" He and George broke into raucous laughter.

Chapter 9

Hannah-Maria!

The barges had gone. The stores had been put away, and Geoff was asking questions of Scotty the cook. Who was she? Where'd she come from? All answers confirmed that she was indeed a phenomenon of nature, and not only in physical appearance. Scotty, with Presbyterian fervor, outlined outrageous gang-bangs, where Hannah-Maria had serviced four or five men, some more than once on the same night; lurid stories about her screwing in the hospital, and "in the kirk by all that's holy!" in the station, in the single men's quarters, and in a scow on the Mackenzie River.

"Hey, where's that photographer guy," Geoff asked. "Wasn't he supposed to have dinner and sleep here tonight?"

But the last Scotty had seen of him, he was heading down the road toward Hannah-Maria's cabin.

"Oh.. And where is that?" was Geoff's last question during the conversation.

Scotty left for his house, and Geoff was alone in the single men's quarters. He tried to read. His self-assigned project was to read all the great books for which he hadn't had time at University. It was also to be as a penance for his apostasy, his desertion of the monastic type of life with which he felt strangely very much at home. If not the whips and scourges of the monk's cell, then long hours of study, his feet in cold water to keep him attentive, while he studied "The Golden Bough".

He was reading the chapter dealing with the influence of the sexes on vegetation. It was perhaps unfortunate-- considering his state of mind-- that he should be reading about ancient and primitive peoples who felt that by having sexual intercourse next to their farms, they could by sympathetic magic, induce good crops. But ah! The twisted course the human mind takes in seeking after truth, for it was pointed out there are just as many cultures that go the other way, proscribing sex completely. Some cultures required the man to leave the woman alone from sowing to harvest time. It was Dionysius versus Apollo all over again.

Geoff made the valiant effort. He tried to concentrate, and when the image of a golden, laughing face, framed in turbulent waves of glistening black hair rose before him he thumped his fists on his desk. "No!" he shouted aloud. It was no good. Images all deriving from that one brief scene by the riverbank kept rising before him, each more voluptuous than the one before.

Finally, he could bear it no longer. He had to see her. All doubts resolved, he sprang up and went out.

The sun was loitering on the horizon. There would be no darkness at all this day. Geoff didn't care. His mind was a torrent of lust that was rushing his brains to the rocks of madness. In an eye-popping stab of déjà-vu, he conjured up a slim, almost stick-like figure, his vow of continence and chastity, being dashed on the rocks, its still small voice, overwhelmed.

He was a man possessed. So he had renounced his vows. Very well, so be it. But his coming down would not be a small transgression, better to rule in hell than serve in heaven! Better to hang as a sheep than a lamb! The blood was coursing through his veins so strongly that it drove him to quicken his pace, then to jog, and finally, to sprint the length of the village till he came to Hannah-Maria's cabin.

He stared at the rough, weather-beaten door. What was he to do now? Simply walk in, knock her down, start biting her soft, pillowy thighs! His fist was thumping on the door.

An aged woman, a crone really, hunch-backed and wrinkled like a bloodhound, opened the door, looked out past him and muttering something he couldn't understand, withdrew to her room and left.

There was muffled sound coming from the other room to the right. Geoff walked over, listened for a minute, and knocked quietly.

"Hanna-Maria!" the sound of his voice startled him. A man lost in the desert, suffering laryngitis and thirst. "It's me, Heironymous Geoff. You know, the new guy up at the weather office. I gotta see you."

"Ah, Nah-ee-sho, come in," a voice answered. Geoff entered. There she was, covered up so that just her head showed. She was in the throes of barely controlled laughter, and seeing Geoff, his face puffy with lust, made her guffaw.

"C'mon and join the party!" she shrilled, and whipped down the caribou-hide coverlet of her bed.

There in a long, woolen union-suit, was Jack Mazooli. Jack glanced nervously about, unsure about what was going on.

"Hi there," he said. "I'm Jack Mazooli, on assignment for MacLean's Magazine."

Hannah-Maria rose from her bed, the clothes falling away to reveal her big, jutting breasts, which jiggled as, laughing still, she gestured to a closet at the side of the small room. Geoff gingerly opened that door to disclose Clarence Clunk, naked as the day he was born, staring about distractedly, for he'd lost his glasses and his hearing aid and batteries lay in disarray at his feet.

Clarence Crunk, the Canadian Pacific Airlines agent at the Fort Poontuk airstrip, was a big man, a fat man, a lethargic, phlegmatic man. He was a sorry memorandum to the proposition that man is mortal and subject to decay: He was almost toothless, had very little hair, wore bottle-bottom-thick glasses and a hearing aid. Besides that his sinuses hurt and he had trouble with his bowels. More than one host on Poontuk had been alarmed with his scatological preoccupations. As a single man, Crunk had often received invitations to dine, but these dwindled; he seemed less concerned about his host's table than his bathroom, to which he invariably repaired upon arrival. After a session of grunting and groaning, sighing and farting, as if he were alone on the tundra, he would emerge to announce that his turds were floating or sinking as the case might be.

But of late, Crunk had sequestered himself at the airstrip in the building provided him there by the airline and rarely came to town. Which was a shame, because Clarence Crunk played a pretty mean fiddle, and he, along with Joe Caribou and his Caribou Rats, would provide music for dances at the recreation hall of the single men's quarters.

"I've been constipated," Crunk announced. "I came in to see doctor Fleming."

Such a sight did he present that Hannah-Maria was almost beside herself with fun. She started pumping her legs as if she were peddling a bike, and slapping her knees with her hands, tossing her head and growling. All three men watched, Crunk with eyes asquint.

When she finally calmed down enough to speak she said, blissfully unaware of her nakedness, "Tree guys... tree guys in here, and not one piece of tail..." And she broke down again, laughing and flung herself back on the bed.

Geoff didn't know what to make of it at first. The girl's laughter contrasted with the wretched state of the men in the room. They stood about like actors in the wings being called upon to perform when they have come to the wrong theatre. Heironymous Geoff trembled at the situation, and then burst into laughter, carrying on until the tears rolled down his cheeks. Mazooli and Crunk saw nothing funny in the situation, and instead, made furtive, desperate attempts to retrieve their clothes and effects.

With Geoff's outburst, Hanna-Maria had stopped and stared incredulously at him for a moment before lapsing again into unbridled hilarity; rocking back and forth on the bed. A baby in the other room started to cry.

"My baby is cryin'," she said, pulling a blanket about herself, and left.

This galvanized the three men into action. They speedily withdrew, saying nothing to the crone, who was now attending something on the stove.

The sun was full and strong. It was warm in Fort Poontuk, as the disparate trio trudged down the road.

Geoff thought: "After coitus, the male animal is gay. But the converse is not true; he's not necessarily happy before sex. As a matter of fact, laughter is the nemesis of lust." He smiled the smile of one who has coined something which he deems is not only witty, but true. He felt strangely "rescued" the ludicrous episode in the cabin had somehow saved him from returning to "the riot and debauchery" that had been his life in Edmonton. His lust had been driven out by laughter; he'd been set back on the path of righteousness by a risible charade. His vow was intact. Hannah-Maria and her sumptuous curves be damned! One must look at life as Scaramouche did, and remember always: "Laugh and the world laughs with you, weep and you weep alone."

His self-indulgent chuckling in meditating on these points failed to communicate to Mazooli and Crunk, who followed morosely behind him. Passing Frank and George's cabin, they heard the pair singing within:

'Amazing Grace, how sweet the sound,
That saved a wretch like me!
I once was lost, but now, I'm found,
Was blind, but now, I see."

Chapter 10

Summer Comes to Poontuk

Summer came on with a rush. In mid-June, Trent and Geoff were surprised to see the thermometer daily scaling to the high seventies and low eighties. Frank and George said this was a good thing. A good hot June would kill a lot of flies. Didn't matter how cold it got, (couldn't you see the fur coats those mosquitoes wore?) heat was the thing to kill the flies. But one would never know this when one ventured into the bush, where the flies pounced on the intruder with savage ferocity, and it was recalled that a former Hudson's Bay clerk, lost in the woods for a scant half-day, had been unrecognizable, and almost out of his mind, when he came stumbling back into Poontuk. But in the cleared part of the settlement itself, life was quiet and pleasant. Signalman Nichol, taking advantage of the twenty-four-hour-a-day sunshine, grew enormous potatoes, carrots, and cabbage in rich soil where, six inches deeper, the earth was permanently frozen.

The native people swelled the population during the summer, coming in from the scattered traplines, and there were many of them who'd never seen snow on the ground in Poontuk.

They gathered for the Tea Dance, a ritual that the whites found baffling. Without any forewarning or obvious preparation, the Indians formed a huge circle. Drummers, wielding moose-hide hoops, gathered in the centre. For days they circled round, listening first to the high-pitched chant of somebody acting the fugleman and then responding in unison, never missing a beat, though before the dance's dispersal, near exhaustion was on the faces of many of the dancers. The drum beats throbbed over the community and the jokes about the natives being restless tonight, frazzled to complaints about the brain punishing monotony of it all.

But as suddenly and mysteriously as it had started, the Tea Dance was ended.

Throughout the summer, there were weekly get-togethers at Harry Crum's hotel, whose chief feature was an auditorium, which would seat the entire population of Fort Poontuk.

There, Joe Caribou and his Caribou Rats would play for square dances and other functions. One such was the jig-dancing contest, which to everybody's amazement, since it was felt her talents lay in other directions, Hannah-Maria always won. While she wasn't given to consorting with her own kind (indulging always the white part of her breeding) the native men could not but admire her wonderful body. While her footwork in the jig-dancing contests left something to be desired, she made up for that in her other parts. Besides, she was required to come back to defend her championship.

She was more attractive than ever. The flattering attentions of Jack Mazooli had buttressed her self-esteem to such an extent she no longer found it necessary to make a brazen self-display. She dressed like the white ladies of the town. She'd also picked up a nickname. Before he left, Mazooli had taken to calling her "Lulu".

After his near fall back into his former life of "riot and debauchery", Heironymous Geoff had settled down with Trent to the business of daily weather reporting and -- while the bottled hydrogen supply lasted -- to upper air observations. These provided entertainment for the natives, who would gather each evening at six to watch Geoff fill one of the big red balloons with gas and release it. They would watch it until, most often at around forty thousand feet, the balloon would burst. Geoff could see through his theodolite, and he was amazed to find that the native population could follow the balloon almost as well with the naked eye. The Indians called him "Nye - EE- Sho", "Balloon Man". As the summer advanced, the exercises at the theodolite became trying. The stationary observer attracted biting insects, which seemed tolerant of every repellant he used. Finally, with the hydrogen all gone, the upper air observations were discontinued. Trent was not happy. He wanted far more information and nagged Nepomuk Permaneder to hurry up with the construction of the hydrogen shed.

Permaneder was taking too long to build the hydrogen shed and it was not to be wondered at. Permaneder started his day, after he'd strapped on his wooden leg, with a pull at a fresh bottle of Johnnie Walker's Red Label. By the end of the working day, the bottle was usually empty, not always because he'd drunk it all, but for his overweening generosity. Never before had Permaneder lived in a place like Fort Poontuk: It was paradise. He set his own hours of work, had good food to eat, lots of whiskey to drink, and the girls were plentiful and sportive. This gladsome condition he shared and celebrated daily, crying: "Haf a drink!" to anyone who came close to his work on the hydrogen shed, as he whipped the bottle from the back pocket of his coveralls. After supper, he was off on a tour of the town. "Teepee creeping" they called it. And Nepomuk's presence could not long be concealed, for the cry: "Haf a drink!" regularly shattered the calm. Constable Button, though fretful of Permaneder's behavior, let him alone. Button explained there would be no charges if he kept his nose clean and didn't get into any trouble with the natives, some of whom were off the "rolls of the band" and therefore eligible to drink, while others, as members of the band, were forbidden. These scruples didn't faze Permaneder, who handed out the whiskey with a lavish hand (he had a case of the stuff coming in every other Friday). He occupied the third room in the single men's quarters and the sleep of the other two occupants, Geoff and Salt, was regularly interrupted by Permaneder's strenuous love making. At times, the entire building shook and made Geoff anxious for the safety of the girl involved. But it was in Permaneder's style. His opening gambit, once the girl was in his room (you could hear it all over the building) was: "How about a little jiggy-jig?" The culmination of the engagement was his loud bellowing: "Oh Ya!" He was so popular with the natives they played tricks on him. Once, when he was shacked up with Hannah-Maria's blondish older sister, some younger brothers mischievously made off with his wooden leg, imprisoning him in the cabin while they rifled his room for his spare whiskey. Meantime, Permaneder woke up and discovering his loss and its consequences, stomped out with a crooked stick for a crutch. He found the boys as they were leaving the premises empty-handed, for he was too worldly-wise to leave the stuff lying about and easily found, and set after them. The boys in turn leapt and ran around the poor German, taunting him with his wooden leg, and jumped, shrieking, out of range when he lunged at them. Many natives turned out to watch and laugh at Permaneder's plight, which went on till the man was gasping for breath. The game might have continued had not Hannah-Maria appeared on the scene. She clouted and tongue-lashed the young tormenters, and restored the leg to its owner.

Chapter 11

Poontuk Panthers - Baseball

It was strongly suspected that a condition of employment among the younger, usually college, men, who applied for summer work on the Northern Transportation Company's boats was that they be good soft-ball players. This was because in fifteen years of competition between the town and the boats, the town had yet to savour victory. Most often the defeats were humiliating. The last one had been fourteen to nothing. But times were looking up, thanks to the Canon Ford, the Anglican Minister stationed in Fort Poontuk. Ford knew the game well, and the annual affair was to take on a new respectability with his coaching: He knew about the infield fly rule[6] and interference by a runner between bases, and he had managed to attract a number of the native men, who, up until then had ignored the practices and games as ridiculous. But Mr. Ford's patience and perseverance paid off when he recruited Joseph and Mary Bourque. "Joseph and Mary" was the man's first name. It was said that he'd been of such a size when born that his mother had given him the double name after expressing surprise she'd not been delivered of twins. Joseph and Mary maintained his early promise, growing into a man of such proportions that, had he been born Outside, he would have become a professional wrestler, star lineman on a football team, or a bone-crunching defense-man at hockey. Alas, Joseph and Mary was not the best coordinated of men. Ford

---

[6] The Infield Fly rule is there to prevent the defense from cheating. The Rule is if there is a pop-up in the infield with runners at first and second, or with bases loaded, and with less than two out, the umpire will signal and call an infield fly if the ball is fair. The runners may advance at their own risk, but the batter is automatically out. It is a rule frequently forgotten by coaches and umpires in the minor leagues.

despaired of ever placing him on the Poontuk Panthers, until one evening at batting practice, Joseph and Mary had unleashed a great blow that sent the ball flying into the forest on the outskirts of the field, a distance Canon Ford measured at five hundred feet. So, Joseph and Mary Bourque became a member of the Poontuk Panthers. Since that time, however; he'd failed to match, or even come close to that feat. But the Canon, despite Joseph and Mary's endless strikeouts and inept performances in right field, kept him on. "There's no defense against the home run," Ford answered his critics.

A week earlier, word had been passed to Fort Poontuk: Get ready! The next boat into the community "The Radium Princess" would have a baseball team ready to defend the Northern Transportation company's unbroken record of victory. Now the Canon was under the gun. He never knew quite what to do in training his team members. Canadians all, they were in bad physical condition, so bad that practice sessions left them stiff and crippled. The first scrub game of the season was usually their best, for after that sore muscles, pulled ligaments, and faint hearts reduced the team to a platoon of hobbling wounded. But this year would be different. The past winter had seen a number of dances and bingos at Harry Crum's place. Harry donated the rent, he was a keen fastball fan, and enough money had been raised to send an order to Edmonton for twenty-five sweatshirts. What a wonderful day it had been when the team took to the field for the first time! A cheer had gone up from the crowd gathered as the team trotted out, resplendent in the black sweatshirts with bold orange lettering, "Poontuk Panthers". With this incentive, the Canon was able to get his club out earlier than usual, and while the usual aches and pains followed, he was hopeful the team, with more practices, would be in good form when the big test came. There was a final practice the day before the boat arrived. It was something less than a success. Button, as the catcher of course, was excellent, but Parnell, the pitcher, complained of a sore arm. First baseman, Andy Sitter, showed up terribly hung over, but it was a long fly ball to right that tried the Canon's patience. Joseph and Mary Bourque was out there, admiring his sweatshirt so intently, he was oblivious to the ball, which almost struck his head. "God, give me strength," said the Canon as he buried his face in his hands.

It was a fine day when the "Radium Princess" arrived. It was eight o'clock in the evening, but the sun was to shine for another five hours. The doughty Panthers were disheartened as the crewmen came ashore. The crewmen were all young, strong and limber, and eager for the fray. They swarmed about, shaking hands with their opponents and wishing them a good game. There was Merton Martin, the pitcher, and best player on the Northern Transportation Company's team. Martin was a man who had deviled the locals before with his superior play. He was fully conscious of his starring role and was starting out, right now, to win. Not for him the friendly intermingling with the other team players: He held himself aloof, a thin patronizing smile on his lips, watching the others with his muscular arms folded across his broad chest.

The whole town had turned out for the big game. It was the event of the Fort Poontuk summer. The trappers and hunters who were gone all winter were there with their wives and children. Patrice Prout of the Hudson's Bay Company and his wife set up a lemonade stand, whose product became quickly "spiked" and doled out free to the crowd. Joe Caribou and his Caribou Rats were there, favoring the fans with their version of "Take Me Out to the Ball Game". Even Clarence Crunk showed up, and after some persuasion, (he'd brought his fiddle with him) joined in. One of the Boy Scout trumpeters at last blew a fan fare to let everybody know the game was about to begin, and a nervous but pleasantly excited Canon Fort estimated the crowd at over one hundred. "The biggest we've ever had," he marveled. Harry Crum called out: "Play Ball!"

Then, instantly, the place became a billingsgate of such ferocity the lead-off batter for the visiting team found two strikes whiffed by him before he could recover from the initial shock of finding himself branded a "dirty, rotten cock-sucker", who after the game would probably "fuck all the girls", besides which he "didn't know his ass from a hole in the ground" and "had shit for brains". Never had the visiting team or newcomers like Geoff encountered such a crowd. The natives felt it was their duty to shout and yell throughout the entire game without fear or favor to either side. Geoff, playing third base, found himself close to the wizened old crone from Lulu's place, who shared a bench with some of the older folk. Throughout the game, she kept up a high-pitched running philippic[7] against him: "Hah! Heironymous Geoff, you got no poop left to play dis game, 'cause yo' been up all night fuckin' Lulu!" and her friends would cackle in agreement.

Good Canon Ford concentrated mightily on the game, as much as anything to keep out the raucous blasphemy that raged about him. Nothing disastrous happened in the first inning. After the shocked first batsman went down, the other two were retired with surprising ease, as they too seemed in a state of shock. It meant that Merton Martin would be the leadoff batter at the top of the second.

When his time came, Martin strode to the plate with a haughty assurance and bravado that cowed the crowd to momentary silence. Sure enough, the first pitch he sent flying out into right field. Big Joseph and Mary suddenly turned his head away to swat at a mosquito, and the ball dropped in for a triple.

[7] bitter verbal attack or denunciation

The crowd went wild.

"Hah! Joseph and Mary yo' ol' sonabits! What da hell yo doin' out dere!"

"Hah!, Joseph and Mary! Why don' you shit out dere. Dat'll drive da mosquitoes away!" For this sally, some wit was accorded a round of cheers and applause.

The next man up singled, and Martin scored the first run. Canon Ford felt the old, sorry record was about to repeat.

But, as the game wore on, surprises were in store for the Panther's coach. Andy Sitter made a diving catch for a third out with two on base, an important play since the ball would have ended up in Joseph and Mary's area. Attracted by the crowd, the flies got worse and bothered the visiting team more, since they hadn't thought to equip themselves with insect repellant. On more than one occasion, some visiting outfielder, waiting for a high fly to fall, couldn't stop swatting at insects and lost the ball. The Panthers were lucky: Centre fielder, Bill Nichol chased a ball that just cleared third base with such ferocity that he overran it. In desperation, he flung his gloved left hand backward and the ball plopped into the pocket. The catch was sensational. The crowd went wild. Panther morale soared. The play retired the side leaving Merton Martin stranded on base. The visitors suddenly realized that they were up against a determined ball-team and not a "stupid bunch of clowns" as Martin had told them.

Between innings, Geoff was seen from time to time talking with "Lulu". This business did not escape the crone, who called out: "What's da matter, Heironymous Geoff, yo' send her to get some French safes for da big party tonight!"

It was the ninth inning. The visitors, now at bat, were leading the Panthers by a score of nine to six. Two visitors were out, but one had reached scoring position at second base, and Merton Martin was up. Martin, a picture of determination, strode to the plate. Just outside the batter's box, he stopped, reached down for some dirt, and rubbed his hands. He stepped up, assumed his stance, and froze into a picture of terrible power. Parnell's first pitch was high and outside, but still as far as Harry Crum was concerned, "Strike One!"

Martin turned about, his lips curled in contempt for this bumpkin umpire. He said nothing. His brilliant blue eyes spoke a message that said, "I'll show you!" Such was his arrogance that he let the next pitch, a tempting one, right down the middle, go by.

"Strike Two!" cried Harry Crum.

All this time, the crowd had been silent. Even the crone had stayed her vile tongue to watch this player, who now had the stage. Merton Martin was not about to let his audience down.

He stepped from the batter's box, stretched the bat behind his back, whirled it spectacularly on high, then, holding the bat at either end, he jumped over it forward and backward, exciting an admiring "Oh!" from the crowd. Now he came forward. Now he thumped home plate, raising a puff of dust. His voice came clear and sharp through the pregnant silence: "Now!"

Geoff leaning over, his hands on his knees at his third base position called out, "Do it now!"

Lulu stepped out from the crowd near third base. All eyes turned and riveted as she stuck out her chest and pulled up her skirt, all eyes except Parnell's. Parnell quickly pitched the ball.

"Strike Three!" bawled Harry Crum.
Livid with rage, Merton Martin flung his bat to the ground and rudely shook off those who tried to calm him down.

"I'll show these donkeys what the game is all about," he raged, as he walked to the mound, smacking the ball into his glove.

He was unnerved. His first pitches were so erratic the

first man was walked, and the second. Then Martin over-reacted, and by pitching too carefully, pitched too slowly, and Appleyard singled. Normally, it would have meant a run, but Sitter, who was beginning to stiffen up, owned himself fortunate to make it from second to third base in time to beat the throw from centre field. The bases were loaded.

Now Joseph and Mary was up. The Canon worriedly rubbed his chin. Merton Martin smiled. He'd seen this big clumsy ox floundering around in right field. Now it was time for some fun. Time to get back at these donkeys.

Martin pitched the ball in a slow, soft curve, the kind one would expect at a girl's school. Joseph and Mary swung mightily, but only stirred the air.

Martin smirked. The crowd sent up a great guffaw, and the shrill voice of the crone could be heard. "Hah! Joseph and Mary, how come you don' use your prick! Forget da bat! You do better with yo big prick!" with her further remarks were drowned out by cheers, jeers and laughter.

The second pitch was fast. The swing this time was so powerfully misdirected that Joseph and Mary spun like a top, his legs twisting like vines. Down he went.

"Strike Two!"

Now Merton Martin was in command. He took his time, looking toward the batter when the ball was returned to him. He touched his fingertips to his tongue, adjusted his cap, hitched up his trousers, and then announced to the batter: "Now, I'm gonna give you a hard, fast one, right down the middle."

"That's what Lulu wants!" cried a voice from the crowd. The crowd quieted down. They watched as Merton Martin went into an elaborate wind-up that signaled a pitch of maximum speed. But at the last instant, there was a change. Martin's hand came to a standstill and the ball, which everyone thought would be bullet-like, floated lazily to the plate. A broad smile of triumph was on Martin's face.

Canon Ford despaired. He watched as his big hitter clumsily drew back the bat, watched as he hunched his shoulders, shuffled his feet, did everything wrong. The Canon buried his head in his hands.

Thump! What was that! Holding his breath, raising his head slowly and deliberately so as not to break the magic spell, the Canon looked up.

Just as slowly a sound came from the crowd, who, like a hydra-headed monster, at first cleared its throat, and then built to an exuberant roar.

For the ball was rocketing up and away. The outfielders stood in wonder and watched the ball pass over them, until it was lost in the forest.

Joseph and Mary flung himself around the bases. His feet were on fire. He jumped, skipped and leaped. He waved his arms and grinned through tears of joy. His teammates clustered round, they jumped on him, shook his hand, patted him, mussed his hair. But suddenly, he brushed them away, Joseph and Mary then raised his outspread hands in a gesture that asked for room, threw back his head, and started to shout his warrior's song. Slowly, others in the crowd joined in, and then a curious thing happened.

Scarcely aware of what they were doing, the whites found themselves joining in a great circle, arms around their neighbor's waists, stamping their feet, circling slowly to the counterpoint of the song and the chant. Canon Ford, Fat Mary, Patrice Prout, Frank and George, Lulu, Bonnycastle, the crone, Sitter, all caught up in a spirit of camaraderie and well-being and perhaps something more; something akin to a celebration of a basic rhythm of mankind, a rhythm that had joined Adam and Eve, and to which only angels and not other species of animals, could respond. It was novel, strange, wonderful for those in the ever-widening circle, as altogether, they stomped their feet and moved to the thump of the hoop drums.

After, few could remember how it had happened that they found themselves with the native Indians, banded together, nor how long it lasted. It was an occasion, a moment, coming from outside normal experience. It was pleasant and relaxing until, like the Presbyterian who went out of curiosity to the Pentacostal revival, he found himself taken in, and the experience was uncomfortable and disconcerting.

Geoff was enrapt in the dance. When the others left, he remained, head thrown back, eyes closed, and arms outstretched, letting the rhythms flow through his body. He felt again the wonder and excitement he had know with the appearance of the Green Flash. If he concentrated hard enough, let the rhythm take his body, he might reach Nirvana! He wished fervently he could join in the falsetto warrior's chant that poured so uninhibitedly from Joseph and Mary's mouth, or the response that rumbled from the natives. But he kept moving away from the total involvement he sought. He finally gave up and went home.

At the single men's quarters, a different kind of celebration was going on. Geoff's opening the door was like the floodgate for pent up shouting, smoke, noise and music. The Fort Poontuk Panthers were hosting their vanquished visitors at an informal smoker, which, considering it was happening between plane days, was a success. Half full bottles had been dug out from nooks and crannies, Nepomuk Permaneder had been persuaded to donate a bottle of his Scotch. Button had managed several bottles of Hospital Brandy from the Brothers at the Hospital, and May Dun had loaned two bottles.

The new Hudson's Bay Clerk was there. Since his arrival, he'd spent most of his leisure time at the single men's quarters. Alastair Robinson, who was quickly nicknamed "Jock" didn't get along too well with Mrs. Prout. She was forever lecturing him on the sins of the community, the fact the girls all had crabs or VD or both, that all the men drank too much, and would he be more careful in removing his "body hair" from the Hudson's Bay company bathtub? So, he spent evenings at the common room, plunking his guitar and singing Scottish laments so repetitively that "John Anderson, My Jo" and "Will Ye No Come Back Again" became the leitmotif for the community. But tonight was different. Jock had unlimbered his bagpipes and was marching grandly up and down the room, blaring away while the others clapped and cheered, or marched with him.

Scotty Lyle was particularly enthused. He lauded the talents of his compatriot. "I wanna sing! I wanna sing", he cried, his eyes welling with tears. "Jock, will ya no gimme a note."

Jock's chanter gave him the keynote for "Sky Boat Song". The party quieted as Scotty cocked his head and sang. It was an ear-grating, discordant rasp. The crowd murmured encouragement: "Try again, Scotty!" "Sure, go ahead, you can do it, Scotty!"

Again, the note sounded from the chanter. Scotty listened, took a deep breath, and with his neck tendons stretching, loosed his second try. It was worse than the first, and a great groan rose from the crowd.

"I can't sing," said Scotty, bursting into tears. "I can't sing."

Well, if he couldn't sing, Scotty could dance. He leaped to his feet and started an inexpert Highland fling, to which Jock added accompanying music. Others joined in, each exhibiting his own brand of the dance until the building rocked.

The dancing became a contest. One by one, men dropped out, until only four remained in the centre of the room, leaping around with more enthusiasm than skill. And then, there were two, Merton Martin and another member of the visiting team, who, goaded by handclapping and the imperious wail of the pipes, whipped themselves into a fury. Finally, the other man fell and Martin stood, clasping his hands above his head in the boxer's victory salute.

Martin looked about him. "Y'know," he said. "We didn't just get beaten by the guys on the Poontuk Panthers. "

Cries of "Poor Sport!" "Sour Grapes!" Crybaby!"

"No, No, wait a minute, hear me out!" Martin continued. "I coulda had a home run, maybe won the game, but I was distracted. Yeah! I was jobbed by a broad with the biggest set of," here he made a gesture round his chest, "and a pair of legs like you never saw. Okay, we lost the game. Can't do anything about that. But I think there oughta be some kind of compensation, and I think that broad is the one to do it."

With that, Matin started for the door. His speech had emboldened some of his mates, who started out with him. "Oh, now, wait boys. I think it's time we pack it in for the night" said Constable Button.

"Ah, c'mon, what's the harm," said Martin. "I'm just gonna go out and look for that broad. She sure gave us plenty of reason to look her up."

"Wait a minute!" Button's voice was growing edgy. I want you all back to the "Radium Princess" and right now!"

"Hey, what do you mean?" said Martin, plainly annoyed. "This is a free country, ain't it? Just because you got a big yellow stripe runnin' down your leg don't allow you to tell us what to do." He became conciliatory. "Besides, there's a little princess right here in this town I'd sooner climb aboard.."

In the chorus of rough laughter that greeted this remark, he brushed by Button and went outside with the others following.

Geoff felt the tension. "They're in an ugly mood. What are we gonna do?"

In ten years with the RCMP, Button had never drawn a gun. But he was worried. "Is there a rifle in this place?" he asked.

Nobody knew. Button was out the door and down the road. He overtook and confronted Martin's group. He held up his hands.

"Okay guys. It's late. The party's over. Let's all call it quits. You can't do anything. A big mob like this isn't going to get anything with the broads. All you can do is get into trouble. It'll be a gang-rape or some bloody thing and I can't let that.."

"Wait a minute! Wait a minute!" shouted Martin. "Where d'you get off tellin' me what to do. I ain't broke the law. And I don't give a good goddamn what these other assholes do, I'm going to do a little visiting."

He and Button stood face to face. It was five o'clock in the morning and the sun was getting warmer.

"C'mon, Martin," said Button. "Don't you be an asshole."

Martin made a shift as though to pass by, or turn away, one couldn't be sure, because a rifle shot thundered over the scene. Then everybody shrank back.

Geoff came forward. He'd located a rifle, and seeing the confrontation, had impulsively fired into the air. Now, the staunch upholder of law and order, "Steel of the Mounted", part of that band who'd run the whiskey-traders from the Northwest Territories, banished the gunslingers, and made the Canadian west such a peaceful place, Geoff handed the rifle to Button.

Button, relieved, amused and grateful all at once could only manage, "Thanks, deputy."

The rifle shot had done the job. Martin and the others stared about at their surroundings and muttered their apologies to Button. Martin seemed about ready to say something to Button, thought the better of it, and waving for the others to follow him, left for the boat and the barges.

The word got around the next day that had it not been for the intervention of "Nye-ee-sho", a whole gang of men would have come to rape Lulu.

Chapter 12

Summer Love

Nobody from the Outside is ever prepared enough to accept the northern seasons. For the greater part of the winter, the sun does not rise. For weeks there is but a faint tantalizing blush on the horizon. Then for the greater part of the summer, the sun doesn't set and the senses become numbed by the constant brightness that in Poontuk revealed only the same shabby cabins, the scrubby forest, with its sparse and unlovely undergrowth, and the vast, brown-grey river, which, like the outer rim of some gigantic wheel, went by quietly and monstrously, day after day. The river was too cold, and the current too strong for swimming. In fact, the river was set apart from human endeavors completely, and it seemed to suffer the barges only because of their infrequency and insignificance. In August, there was a period in Fort Poontuk that resembled the typical day on the Outside. The sun went down at night and rose in the morning, and while the dark hours were brief, they tended to bring a sense of normalcy. There were other things as well. Radio reception in the late summer and early autumn was better, and the women regularly gathered on Mondays for "Lux Radio Theatre" while the men augmented their regular Thursday poker night with a Monday one. On the former occasion however, they were required to baby sit, and the single men's quarters on Monday nights became a care centre for the town's white infants and toddlers, of which there were plenty.

Throughout the summer, work had progressed on the weathermen's hydrogen shed. Nepomuk Permaneder said he would have it finished before the snow flew, and Trent was happy to hear that. Trent was beginning to wonder if Nepomuk would ever finish the job.

Trent was worried. There were signs that the forthcoming winter would be a particularly severe one: There was a massive and extremely cold high pressure system already building in Siberia, and this would ultimately affect Alaska and Canada. It would also make the occurrence of Trent's sought-after warm wind very unlikely.

Geoff was tiring of the endless columns of figures Trent gave him to add and summarize. There'd been a slip up somewhere, and an adding machine, which was to have come to Poontuk, somehow ended up at the two-man station at Alert Bay, the northernmost weather station in Canada. Repeated requests to the authorities in Edmonton for the adding machine always brought the same reply: Poontuk has an adding machine, it was sent on the first boat of the season. There were papers to prove it. Which meant that Geoff was required to add columns of thirty or thirty-one five-figure numbers twenty-four times, since barometric pressure readings as well as temperature, humidity, wind-speed, and other meteors, were now being done on a twenty-four hour basis. All these data had to be averaged and abstracted for Trent, who sought to find some pattern, some key that would unlock the door to the mystery of the warm winds. But the exercise was dull as dishwater for Geoff. He found that work at the weather office was dulling his brain and killing his imagination. His painting, his notes on the great classics were beginning to suffer. Geoff felt squeezed out, dried up. Only occasionally did he wake up with that chest-thumping lust for life he once felt every day; an euphoria that would drive him skipping onto the road where he would race up and down, singing to the sky in pure animal good spirits. This didn't happen anymore, or very seldom, thanks to Trent and his soul-destroying numbers. Geoff decided he would never make a forecaster.

The routine changed abruptly one day. It was a quiet day in the common room. Geoff and Salt were reading magazines, when Scotty, rolling his eyes and smirking, announced that Geoff had a visitor. It was Lulu, and she'd changed. She was dressed in a conservative maroon-coloured suit with a white blouse and scarf; her hair had been done, and at her side was her oldest daughter, a child of about five. Lulu came in like some grande dame out for afternoon tea. The total effect, because it was so unexpected, was dumbfounding. Lulu and her daughter sat down on the chesterfield.

"What's da madder, Heironymous Geoff, don't you like me anymore?" was Lulu's opening statement.

Geoff was at a loss for words.

"You never come to see me after da ball game," she said. "After you asked me to show off like dat, I tot you really liked me, but I guess you don't, eh?"

She kept her mouth open and moistened her lips while staring at him.

"Oh yeah, well, you see Lulu, it's just that I've been busy at the weather office, and workin' hard and all that.."

"How about I come and see you Friday night?"

"Well, I..."

"Okay, Heironymous Geoff," and with that she got up to leave. "Be round 'bout eight o'clock." She took her daughter by the hand and left.

Geoff was left standing. "What the hell?" he muttered. He looked in question at Scotty, who'd been listening by the kitchen door, but Scotty only shrugged.

"What does she mean she's going to visit me?" wondered Geoff. "We're not going to bloody-well play cards, that's for sure. She's coming here to get laid!"

He paced about the common room. His buttocks started to tingle; he felt new life in his loins. What was he doing with his life? It had been sidetracked into a sterile exercise of numbers, counting and dilettantism. Why, in trying to live the life of a monk, he'd squelched his own spirit. That was why he didn't feel like jumping up and singing in the morning. That was why he felt defeated, dull and stupid most of the time. He didn't talk anymore because he had nothing to talk about. He didn't celebrate life because he was denying it. He would change. Lulu was his succubus, come to rescue him from corrupting moth and rust. He would live. "The road of excess leads to the palace of wisdom!"

It was Friday evening, two days after Lulu's visit. Geoff saw a devilish design in her invitation, because in those ensuing two days he'd built him self up into a towering state of horniness. He hadn't slept last night, he'd been haunted by visions of plump thighs and breasts, jet-black hair being tossed about while laughing red lips rippled over flashing white teeth. He waited till half-past eight in the common room, then returned to his room and flung himself down onto his bed. He was tortured by the thought she wouldn't show up. His testicles were aching. He was biting the pillow when he heard a giggle from under the bed. It was she.

"What!" gasped Geoff.

"I just came in da window," she smiled and unbuttoned a caftan-like garment, to reveal herself totally naked.

Staring at him, she moistened her lips again and joined him on the bed. They kissed.

She looked amused. "Do you always like da dry kiss, Heironymous Geoff?" she asked.

She pulled his face down and plunged her tongue deep inside his mouth. He jumped on her.

"Take it easy, take your clothes off," she scolded. At the first touch of her bare body, he ejaculated, squirting all over her thighs.

"You're hotter dan a two-dollar shotgun, Heironymous Geoff! You wouldn't leave a girl high and dry...huh?" Then she leaned over him and expertly brought Geoff to his former state, starting first by tiny kisses along his hair-line, roving her tongue along his eyebrow, pecking at the corners of his mouth, and proceeding so that before Lulu's visit concluded, her ministrations and Geoff's enthusiasm brought him to the ecstatic state five times. After Geoff had walked her home, he returned to confide in his journal, "I might truly style myself a man of pleasure."

Geoff's playing at monkery had had an effect not unlike the northern climate, swinging from one extreme to the other. Geoff and Lulu made love almost every night in his room. On Mondays and Thursdays, when men gathered for poker, they found other places. Nothing was ever locked in Poontuk. So they grappled in the diesel shed, Harry Crum's hotel, in the fur storage room at the Hudson's Bay Post, in Bill Nichol's root cellar, and even on Button's living room rug one Thursday when the constable was playing poker. With the women gathered in one home, they would invade one of the deserted ones.

Geoff's summer went by in a fog of concupiscence. He seemed to be either having sex with Lulu or thinking about it. Those evenings when he waited for her in his room were an agony. He though he'd go mad if she didn't show up. The thought of her body drove all other thoughts out. Raphael said a masterpiece is that work of art on which the imagination cannot possibly improve. Then, her body was a masterpiece. Geoff made an effort to render her likeness as an academic nude. But Lulu wasn't enthusiastic about posing, and she told him she thought it was a waste of time. She had only to wriggle her breasts or hips to get him to fling his brushes aside and come fairly leaping at her; she only had to open her mouth and lick her lips to bring him to an erection. She was a succubus without which Geoff would die. Her smile became like a symphony to him: the adagio, a slow smooth wave rippling from the centre to the corners of her wide, generous lips; andante, a gradual, slow parting to reveal her big white teeth; scherzo, the full blaze of her smile, something that started as a smile of almost girlish innocence and then changed to a finale of animal wantonness. In the act of sex, he would hear the trios of the various movements of Beethoven's Third Symphony resounding in his mind's ear; the initial thrusts timed to those two slashing chords that open the symphony, followed by the lyrical variations whose drive almost brought him to the climax. Then he could settle down to march through the funereal part and gather strength for the pattering short jabs of the scherzo. He never made it to the finale, even though the piece was rendered two and sometimes three times a night.

But Geoff could not dabble with these conceits for long. Lulu's sexual appetite was ravenous. She was at him three or four times a night every night for weeks, in his room or any of their other trysting places. She wanted him to spend the night in her cabin; love was so much more fun in the morning after a night's rest, she said. But he found the idea repugnant with the two children there and the crone skulking about the place. Attempts to satisfy only increased her hunger. At the Hudson's Bay Post, while he was waiting to pay for a purchase and Mr. Prout was temporarily out of the room, she came in, placed herself before him and ground her buttocks into his loins, assuming the picture of innocence when Mr. Prout reappeared. She sneaked in while Geoff was doing his weather data abstracts and after unbuttoning her clothes, lowered herself upon him while he still sat in the chair. Or she would fling herself face down upon the table, wiggling her buttocks and hitching up her skirt to reveal their nakedness. Her daring and ingenuity in these matters were remarkable. She seemed to spend her every waking moment planning them.

The old crone was her grandmother, worn out by the rough, harrowing life on the trap line for a succession of husbands. Lulu's parents were God knows where. It was her uncle, Felix, who'd more or less brought her up.

Uncle Felix was one of those who'd made something out of himself. He not only ran a trap line, but he had employment as a welder down river at the great Imperial Oil installations at Norman Wells. He was becoming something of a legend along the river, making so much money that he'd recently bought a diesel tractor, after first taking a course in Edmonton on how to run it. He could see big things happening in the north once the affairs of the War, now two years passed, were settled. Geoff had seen uncle Felix in Poontuk once. He was a short, intense, wiry little man, who'd strode into a group of Indians idling around the ramp of a barge, ordered them to do this and do that, and in no time had them whipped into a hard-working gang. His eyes, in the deep bronze of his face, were strikingly blue, cold, penetrating, and absolutely merciless. Lulu had to watch out for Uncle Felix, who as her mother's half-brother, had appointed himself her guardian. As such, he let it be known he was not happy about Lulu's venery, her two illegitimate kids or her shiftlessness. It was Uncle Felix who'd raised the matter of Lulu's infidelities with the RCMP, and while Button had told him there was little that could legally be done, the policeman passed the word around to everybody to "lay off Hannah-Maria". He was prepared to do anything for peace and good order in the community.

Geoff couldn't have cared less about Uncle Felix. He was going blind! At first, he tried to tell himself the print in his books was defective, or the light wasn't right, but there was no denying that his eyes were becoming blurry and itchy. He told nobody about it, not even Lulu, and when he was not with her, he was brooding about his eyesight. Finally, one day, he went over to visit old Dr. Fleming.

Lulu was languidly rubbing her foot up and down the length of Geoff's naked leg, tickling his foot with her toes and sticking her tongue in his ear.

He sighed. "Do you realize," he said solemnly, "that

because of your never-ending sexual demands, I'm slowly going blind."

She propped herself on an elbow, and leaned over to him. "Bullshit," she said.

"No, no bullshit." How he hated language like that. "I was over to see doctor Fleming today, and he told me I've a condition known as 'post-marital ambylopia'."

"Bullshit!"

"What the hell do you know about it?" responded Geoff. "I'm telling you, that's what the Doc said. Said it's a condition that affects a lot of guys after they get married. They go at it so hard that they go blind. That's right. Oh, you can laugh if you like, but I'm telling you the truth. 'Post marital ambylopia', that's what the Doctor said."

"Hey, Heironymous Geoff, can you see dis?"

"Oh, now, Lulu, for God's sake, cut it out!"

"You can see it all right, so you're not blind yet." She chuckled quietly and moved toward him. "Let me on top dis time."

The lovemaking over, she said: "You know, Heironymous Geoff, I tink your trouble is you read too much."

There was a welcome respite when Canon Ford started his rehearsals in early September for his production of "The Bishop's Candlesticks". Geoff was puzzled at his own behavior. Thinking back on the excitement the sight of Lulu's body had given him, it now seemed inconceivable that he now sought ways to avoid her.

Chapter 13

Summer's End

Rehearsals for the play were held in the auditorium of Harry Crum's Hotel, and were intellectually and socially refreshing for Geoff. If he ignored Mrs. Prout, who was typecast as a nagging old shrew, the company was good; Canon Ford, Jean Trent, and Constable Kenneth Button. It was stimulating to discuss character development, the "spine" or main theme of the play and, evening after evening, they sat about discussing the inter-relations of the various characters and how these might be fused for the greater dramatic force of the whole play. Talk, talk, talk, the very thing that was Geoff's meat and drink, when he could discuss such open-ended topics as "motivation", "Stanislawsky method", "theatricality", and "stage presence".

"Well, really, Jerome," said Mr. Ford. "I don't think we need delve into the subject quite that deeply. This is a one-act play that will probably be over in twenty minutes, and only aims to teach the power of Christian forgiveness. It's not Shakespeare, just a simple, little one-act play that carries a very important message.

"But for me, it's not as simple as that, Mr. Ford," said Geoff, his eyes gleaming. "Sometimes, when we're rehearsing on that stage, I begin to feel I'm losing my own identity, you know, that I'm becoming the man I'm playing."

"Oh, for heaven's sake, Jerry," said Jean Trent. "You've got about a half-dozen lines. I don't see how that's such a big deal. How can you lose your own personality and become someone else in such a small part?"

"There are no small parts, only small actors."

"Oh, shut up!"

Paul Salt showed up for rehearsals explaining he'd like

to help out with the props and scenery. After a time, Oscar Appleyard, who had a good collection of carpenter's tools, came to help out. Mr. Ford was delighted and made plans to have the play put on in the Christmas season as part of a Gala Christmas Concert to be held in the same auditorium.

After rehearsals, Geoff and Appleyard, almost as a matter of routine, got drunk.

"I know what you're going through," confided red-haired, snaggle-toothed, Appleyard. "My wife's a half-breed herself and…" He snickered and raised his voice so that it carried to his wife in the bedroom, ".. all those half-breeds are holy terrors. Wear a man out! From what you tell me, Jerry, you're lucky to still have your eyesight. Hah Hah! Here, have another short, sharp reading." He passed the rum bottle.

Geoff was drunk when he reached the door of the single men's quarters. He staggered inside, knocking over the garbage and sending a thousand tin cans crashing across the floor. "Ganymede returns!" he announced to the darkness, and giggled.

The kitchen lights turned on. It was Lulu.

"Drunk again, eh?" she said. She strode forward and socked him on the jaw.

Geoff was stunned. "Hey, what gives?"
Her hard little fists were thumping about his head and shoulders. He'd never seen her like this.

"Comin here drunk all da time, dat's what you're doing, Heironymous Geoff," she said, almost in tears, frustrated by his warding off her blows. She was surprisingly strong. "Oh, you", she wailed. "I tot we had a love for each udder. But now you actin' like we was married. You go out and get drunk and won't come back."

"I was at a rehearsal for that play"

"Dat doesn't take to tree o'clock in da morning," she said, wiping tears from her cheeks. "And I was here all dat time. Mr. Salt was dere too, but he got home around half-past ten. I've been sittin' here since before dat, but you just go out and get drunk and don't care about me."

"Now, wait a minute. Don't get all worked up again," said Geoff, bringing his hands up to his face protectively.

Lulu moved closer toward him. She studied his face and smiled. Heironymous Geoff was not good looking. He had a cocked eye, but the imperfection, particularly when he was enthused and his eyes blazed, was endearing. He had freckles, more on the right side than on the left side of his face, giving him an unfortunate piebald look. Geoff was so blissfully unaware of the condition, or at least ignored it so completely, that persons meeting him were immediately charmed and put at ease.

She was speaking quietly now. "You know, da first time I saw you was when you ran out on da river dat time. My goodness! Dat was really brave. Everybody was talkin' 'bout it. Den I heard about you savin' me from all doze guys who were going to come and try to rape me after da ball game. I tot you really liked me. Why do you have to get drunk all da time?"

"I'm pretty drunk right now. D'you think I can get it up?"

"We won't know if we don' try," she said.

Next rehearsal, Lulu was there. She took it upon herself to make coffee for the players after they'd finished and even brought round some cookies that she'd made herself.

"But, Hannah-Maria, they're delicious," said Jean Trent. "You must give me the recipe some time."

Lulu smiled and whispered her "Thank you". It was confounding to Geoff, who kept up the pretense of just being 'friends' with Lulu. How desperately shy she was in front of white people. She was two completely different persons: the exhibitionist, the fiery nymphomaniac he took to bed or table or whatever ten times a week, and this shy, blushing young woman who scarcely spoke above a whisper, and who on this occasion, jumped up and ran back to the kitchen to brew more coffee.

"My, my, my, " sighed Jean Trent to her retreating figure. "I wish I had a figure like that. I wonder how she keeps it?"

Jean was tempted to turn to Geoff and say, "I'll bet you keep her in shape, " but thought better of it. She and all the others in Fort Pooktuk joined in the conspiracy of not talking about Jerome Geoff and Lulu Burns. It was a ridiculous situation that made Geoff smile to himself. The smile would vanish though, when he wondered as to the reasons for the conspiracy. Then Uncle Felix's blue, merciless eyes would flash on the inward eye.

The brief summer of Fort Poontuk was coming to an end. The last boat, the last soft ball game of the season went by, and on the last day of August, a snow flurry hit town. The snow didn't last. It was a mere touch of white powder. But it reminded everybody that winter was not far off. The dogs in the town sensed they were about to be put to work soon, and their restlessness, yips, yowls, growls, howls and chain-rattling, regularly swept through the town with the frequency of waves on a seashore. There was no change in the forest, no sudden blaze of golden, autumnal glory, for the forest only got darker, more menacing. The air, no longer scorched on a twenty-four hour basis by the sun, smelled purer and cleaner, and the flies were not so bothersome. High in the sky geese were flying south, evoking with their moving, calligraphy and distant cries, an order and system outside man's experience. On the horizons round about, the slate grey curtains that lay rolled throughout the summer were now lowered.

Scows, equipped with outboard motors (kickers these were universally called down north) still raced about on the river. None went so fast or was on the river so often as

Canon Ford's. The Canon's prowess at handling the scow in the heavy Mackenzie current was admired by all, even by the Indians who were to the river born. Ford liked to take trips across the river to a tributary stream, where Arctic char or grayling could be caught. Though most often the catch was Northern Pike or Ling Cod.

Ford would come back slowly, the motor idling, so he could feel the strength and press of the mighty Mackenzie on the rudder and the shudder of the scow. If he were to shut off the motor completely, the river would bear him out of sight of Fort Poontuk within minutes in its headlong rush to the Arctic Ocean. Because this was the business of the river: To ravage the north for its water, draining the biggest lakes in the world and the numberless smaller ones, stretching dendritic tentacles to claw and rob every drop of moisture from every parched acre of the north. To return it all to the Arctic Ocean, to the ice pack. What a waste! There was more water passed by Fort Poontuk in a few minutes than would sustain the population of the largest city for a day, and all that water bound for the Arctic Ocean. All the eager scavenging of lakes, streams, snow and rainfall was all directed not southward to the people and the warmth, but north, to the ice pack. The Arctic is a desert. The precipitation more like the Sahara than even the Prairies, and yet the Mackenzie took what moisture was left after the last encroachment of the Ice Pack and returned it. There are longer rivers than the Mackenzie, and these provide a stimulus and avenue for human intercourse. The Saskatchewan-Nelson system brought the first white people westward across the continent. Rivers nurture towns, cities, whole civilizations, delivering goods, carrying off waste, fertilizing fields, linking communities, inspiring poets and reminding all of the tyranny of time. Not the Mackenzie. Nothing warm or lazy or human about the Mackenzie: Cold, wide and deep, it rolled by in complete disdain of the unlovely communities that clung to its banks, interested only in getting back home to the ice.

Canon Ford had never seen Trent speak so long or so energetically as when he asked: "Are we in for another ice age?"

"Depends on what scientist you talk to," Trent smiled. "I know, that's a typical weatherman's hedge, but in trying to answer a question like that, it's justified. Anyway, all seem to agree that an Ice Age only comes with a warming up in the Arctic Ocean, maybe even the opening up of a third coastline for Canada in the Arctic. In order to bring on a new Ice Age, there has to be much heavier snowfalls than the Arctic gets right now over a very long period of time, centuries even. In order to get this heavier snowfall, there has to be greatly increased evaporation, which doesn't happen as long as the polar Ice Pack is there. Melt that, start the evaporation, and I know this sounds like a contradiction, on comes the ice age.

"Sam, you talk about the river and the way it seems to be carrying half the water in Canada back to the ice pack. I haven't thought about that. All I can tell you is, Mackenzie River nor no, we've got to have a warm-up in the arctic. It's a meteorological thing, and of course, that's where the arguments start. Some have statistics to show it's warming up, others say it's really cooling off. The present warm up is an aberration against the grain. God knows the weather has been cold enough around here in 'forty-five and 'forty-six, so who's to say. Anyway, nothing stays the same. Since the formation of the earth the evidence is that the world has been warmer than it is now. The glaciations that moved across Canada are the exceptions rather than the rules. There's still about ten percent of the last glacier left and maybe this time, when it goes completely, it won't mean the start of another glacial period. Maybe it'll just bring Canada back to normal. Warm enough to grow dinosaurs! Only, don't hold your breath. The last glacier started its retreat, as far as we can estimate, about eighteen thousand years ago. This isn't bad going when you consider it was up to two miles thick in places. But here again, the warm-up hasn't been constant. The climate around Lake Superior, for God knows what reason, was warmer three thousand years ago than it is right now. The trend in the Canadian climate right now seems to be going downhill, I mean, and only roughly speaking, we should expect much colder winters and hot drier summers, at least until the end of this century. Statistically speaking of course. There are always the things that don't fit."

Trent, enthused, was transformed into a much younger man.

Canon Ford was impressed. "Cutting through all the ifs and buts I'd say you've confirmed what I felt when I was on the river yesterday. The trend is toward cold and darkness. Let's hope that the forecast is like most you weathermen give; at best, a good guess.

"Agreed, said Trent. "Man proposes, God disposes!" With that, the two men bowed to each other like on-stage vaudevillians.

There were meteorological phenomena of more immediate impact on Fort Poontuk. Trent's charts showed a high-pressure system settled on the Arctic Ocean. After assuming protean shapes duly noted in the charts, the high coalesced into a closed system like a wheel turning clockwise and bringing easterly winds to the Poontuk district. Strange things happened. Dark, glowering clouds built back from the Mackenzie mountains as the wind climbed, cooled and condensed upon them. With the wind continuing, smoke from the never-ending muskeg fires to the East was carried in and a fine ash filtered down gently all day and night, day after day from the soot-grey cloud. The weather shut out the sky, and encapsulated the community in a cocoon of gloaming dusk. One couldn't see across the river, and the sun disappeared, leaving only an eerie, surreal glow, as if from the substance of the cloud itself. There were no shadows. The settlement reached an hiatus. The funereal weather robbed people of incentive and energy. Like madmen, everybody withdrew into themselves. If they moved or spoke at all, it was done quietly, fearful of terrible consequences should the mood be shattered. The weather dictated a philosophy smacking of Taoism: 'the greatest good is to do nothing',

The rehearsals were suspended. Nepomuk Permaneder could be heard snoring the late afternoons and the nights away. Geoff and Lulu, after the rabid zeal of their earlier encounters, settled down to a fornicatory routine. She even took time out to launder his shirts and underwear and once, instead of jumping into bed, set about cleaning up his room.

"What makes you so ambitious?" asked Geoff. "Everybody else in this town is practically dead. So am I. It's the weather."

"We've had wedder like dis before," she replied. "I gotta clean up here 'cause it's startin' to smell like a fish shed."

"Well, you can hardly blame all that on me," he said, watching her body moving in the plain house dress. "C'mon to bed."

"No, I'm gonna finish up first."

"I'd love to take you away and live together in a cabin somewhere, then we could make love night and day."

"You'd get tired of it," she snapped. She put aside the broom. "Listen, Uncle Felix is coming one of deze days. When he comes here, don't do nutin', I'll tell you what to do."

"Uncle Felix again. Who the hell is he anyway?"

"He's bad" responded Lulu. "Killed a guy, once."

Chapter 14

Uncle Felix

Trent had called a meeting at the station. All the Signalmen turned out for what Trent said would be a "briefing" on what he expected of them during the coming winter. He'd received some new thermometers, which were good for any degree of cold. He had robot thermometers set up on the slopes of the Mackenzie mountain range, and there'd be twice daily balloon observations that would begin when Nepomuk Permaneder finished the hydrogen shed.

"And I hope Nepo," said Trent, "That you'll lay off the local squaws long enough to give us two honest day's labor put together."

Some of the men snickered.

"Dat's okay," said Nepomuk, righteously. "All you guys is married. You come home from work and you got it right there!" He gestured with a grasping, outstretched hand. "Single guys like me, we gotta get out and hustle for it."

Then Lulu appeared in the door. As always, her appearance set off whistles and comments, and she blushed crimson at seeing all the men. But she didn't run away. She hung her head and went to Geoff's side.

She spoke in a heavy, leaden voice, which, at least to Geoff, thundered around the room. "I won' come tonight. Uncle Felix is here."

She left, her wake punctuated by laughs and catcalls. "Who's Felix? The Cat?"

"Somebody let the cat outa the bag, Geoff"

"Is he the one with the shotgun, Jerry?"

"Anyway, it'll help your eyes!"

This last remark brought a roar of approval.

Uncle Felix was there when Geoff returned to the common

room later that evening. Felix wore a denim shirt and trousers outfit, like a cowboy, with tight black gloves, which he tightened across his knuckles.

"Your name Jerry Geoff?" he asked. His voice, like the eyes, steely cold.

"Yes," responded Geoff. "What can I do for you?"

Felix smiled a thin smile. Though smaller than Geoff, one felt the presence of coiled, still springs and murderous, sharp points. "I think you know what it is you can do for me."

A long pause. "Well," Geoff said.

"Lookit, you don't play cute with me," the words came from Uncle Felix's mouth as from a machine gun. "I think you oughta know, and know damn good, that if you get Hannah-Maria in trouble, you're in trouble. Know what I mean? She's already had two illegitimate kids and the guys who did it couldn't care less. They're outside somewhere, spendin' money and gettin' more easy fuckin' .. just like you. Well, it ain't gonna happen again. Know what I mean?"

Geoff was intimidated. He swallowed hard and blurted, "She's no business of yours. She's twenty-one years old and quite capable of looking after..."

"Mr. Geoff!" Uncle Felix's blue eyes blazed. "Lemme show you somethin'."

He took a beer bottle cap out of an ashtray. He held it up between thumb and forefinger, and, as Geoff watched, he folded it neatly in half. He tossed it to Geoff.

"That to your balls!" said Uncle Felix. He turned and left.

Geoff stood for a moment, stunned. The first cognate emotion was anger. Geoff paced up and down in the common room, smashing a fist into his open palm and raging: "That rotten son of a bitch. Who does he think he is? I should have told the bastard where to get off! I should have told him that Lulu and I will continue to see each other.

I mean, what legal or any other rights has he got anyway?"

Then, the blue eyes flashed with animal rage before him, and he heard Lulu's voice: "He's bad. He killed a guy once."

For several days, he saw nothing of Lulu, and busied himself at the weather office, catching up on all the weather summaries and abstracts, and amazing Trent with his energy and initiative.

"I'm sublimating," he explained mysteriously to Trent, as he dashed out to help Nepomuk with the construction of the hydrogen shed.

After several days, he suffered frustrations of a different kind. He wanted Lulu badly, but she seemed to take sadistic pleasure in his condition. He'd been talking to Canon Ford in front of the Hudson's Bay store when Lulu approached with her Uncle. She was a vision of carnal beauty. Geoff's mouth went dry at the sight of her.

"Hey, Heironymous Geoff, I hear yo' eyesight's gettin' better," she said, flashing him a voluptuous smile, just before her uncle jerked her away.

"You've been having trouble with your eyes?" Ford inquired.

"Yes, yes," responded Geoff, full of anxiety. "But I'm okay now."

He tried to paint. He tried to write. He tried, hour after hour, to unhitch his mind from the black horse that roved Lulu's body and bury it in the last chapters of "The Golden Bough". It was useless. As often as not the trios from Beethoven's Third would thunder through his head.

He suddenly sang out: "Sometimes, I wish that I had never met you!" and from the next room, Salt called out, "Will you keep it down? What's the matter? You goin' nuts?"

'That's right,' thought Geoff. 'I'm going mad. I wonder if anyone has ever gone mad out of sexual frustration. But of

94

course, it happens all the time. The dirty old men who "flash" in front of women. They're frustrated. Guys who steal women's panties off clotheslines, or guys who shove needles up their scrotums, who jerk off all the time...'

He got out of bed and opened a copy of MacLean's magazine. It had come in on the last plane, and he hadn't looked at it.

There was a full-page picture of Lulu! Geoff's eyes popped. He was genuinely surprised. Mazooli had been as good as his word, and better. Here she was in the notorious skirt and sweater, smiling benignly from the banks of the Mackenzie. The caption read: "Lulu Burns of Fort Poontuk, N.W.T. watches as the season's first barges reach her community. Miss Burns is typical of the young women in Canada's north.

"Hah, typical!" snorted Geoff. "Typical like Helen of Troy, Aphrodite, Venus!"

Surprise and curiosity at seeing her picture was now driven out by a pang of intense desire. There was an added dimension to her now. Lulu, the girl he had slept with nightly was of such beauty that national magazines ran full page pictures of her. At this very moment, thousands of men were lusting over it.

"But she's mine!" shouted Geoff.

From the next room came Salt's voice: "What the fuck's the matter now?"

Geoff didn't answer. He would go down to Lulu's. Show her the picture. Hell, her Uncle Felix couldn't object to that. If he played his cards right, he might be able to work something out. Get Felix off his back. He could see them all..he, Felix and Lulu, gathered around the table at Lulu's kitchen, and by the light of the Coleman lamp, leaf through the magazine. And perhaps Lulu's cool, tender hand would slyly reach out and touch him on the thigh.

He was out the door. Had to stop, rush back in and

pick up the magazine and start off again. Lulu's cabin was near the downstream end of the village, about a quarter-mile off. It was dark, so he broke into a run. He dashed by Frank and George's cabin. They could be heard "revivaling" again:

"Yield not to temptation,
For yielding is sin,
Each Victory will help you,
Some other, to win..."

... soon their voices were lost in the dogs' noise and chain rattling.

He was at Lulu's door. He paused for a moment to catch his breath and decide on his next move. His legs decided it for him. They carried him past the door and into the kitchen area.

There was no one in the kitchen.

"Hello," he called softly. "Anybody here?"

The Coleman lamp hissed above the stove. He called again.

No answer.

He moved to the door of her bedroom, opened it and peeped in. Her bed was empty and against it at the foot was the baby's crib with the infant sleeping soundly. Lulu couldn't be far.

Then he heard voices and distinctly the nasal staccato of Uncle Felix. What to do? It was too late to run out front and so far as he knew, there was no other exit. Gone was the original thought that had brought him here. As quickly and as quietly as he could, he slid down under Lulu's bed.

They came in and closed the door. Someone, he supposed it was the old crone, went to the stove and fussed about. They would be having tea. Lulu's older child, the daughter, came into the bedroom. She reached under the bed and with a practiced hand, grasped the po, which lay near Geoff's feet. He cringed into the corner while his flesh started to creep. The child urinated and pushed the po back under the bed. It struck Geoff's knee. In the next moment, the young girl was staring him in the face in the dim light.

He said nothing. He made a shift to flicker his fingers, and he smiled. The young girl quickly smiled back and left.

"This is it," thought Geoff. "This is where that homicidal maniac makes it number two."

A surprised shriek came from the old crone. "Ah, Hannah-Maria!" she cried.

What was going on! Geoff had almost decided to leave his hiding place, but he was deterred. Nobody came crashing into the room. They were engaged at something in the main kitchen part of the place. He could hear rustling of paper and exclamation. They'd found the magazine. He searched about him. He'd dropped it in the kitchen.

The three of them, Lulu, Felix, and the crone were talking in a peculiar tongue that seemed compounded of Slavey Indian, some French and a smattering of English idioms. But, judging from the tenor of the questions and the answers, it seemed that Lulu had convinced them she had got the magazine and had forgotten about it until now.

"Pourquoi?" that was Uncle Felix.

"Parce-que je suis très modèste, " Lulu sang out blithely and they all laughed.

"Mama, Mama!" it was the child. Geoff could imagine her tugging at her mother's sleeve, pleading for attention. Then he heard Lulu say, "Well, what is it?"

"In da bedroom, Mama"

She same in and after being directed by the child, looked under the bed. She reacted just like her daughter: With complete nonchalance.

"What is it, Hannah-Maria?" asked the crone.

"It's dis po. It's just about all filled up with piss. Come with me."

She and her daughter left taking the po with them.

How long Geoff waited in his cramped hiding place he

could not tell. It seemed like hours before the crone and Uncle Felix finally turned in. At last, Lulu came into her room. She closed the door quietly, and quickly dropped her clothing to the floor. She lay on the bed.

"Come," she said.

The baby started to cry. It was another half-hour of fussing with bottles, changing diapers and rocking before the baby went back to sleep.

He kissed her at last. Her mouth was warm and soft and moist and yielded completely to his ardent attack. His hand searched below the covers and moved between her thighs. Their mouths mashed.

He climbed upon her. The bedsprings shrieked like banshees.

"Be quiet, be quiet, don't move or nuthin'" she whispered in his ear.

"What'er we gonna do, what'er we gonna do?" hissed Geoff. He made another move, but the bed shrieked again.

"Don'!" she hissed back.

"Hannah-Maria!" Felix's hard, cold voice ripped through the place. "You all right? What's going on in there?"

It sounded like he was going to come in.

"Stay way!" Lulu ordered. "I'm all bare naked and I'm gonna go outside to the shithouse. My kidney's botherin' me."

"It's no wonder."

Lulu got up, wrapped herself in a blanket, and looked into the kitchen, turned and beckoned Geoff to follow.

In all this life, Geoff had never passed over ten or fifteen feet with such fear and trepidation. For there was Felix, his face to the wall, dozing, on the other side of the kitchen.

They were outside.

"C'mon," said Geoff. "Let's go to my place."

"Yo crazy? I got no clothes on and Uncle Felix knows I'm just going dere." She indicated the outhouse. "Come on."

"What? What? Who's the crazy one? We can't do it in that place!"

"Why not?" she said, pushing him inside and perching him on the edge of the outhouse seat. She was grinning impishly, her black eyes flashed as she went about the preparations with speed and enthusiasm. She was humming and chortling as she got him to drop his pants and shorts.

The blanket fell off and her buttocks, two pale, plump moons in the feeble starlight, glimmered, then moved toward him, settling in his lap.

"C'mon," she urged. "Get goin'. We ain't got all night."

When it was over, Lulu was laughing. "With all dat moanin' dat was going on, people will tink I got the constipation!"

Her smile faded. "Heironymous Geoff, listen to me. Uncle Felix gonna take me and da kids back with him to Norman Wells. He wants me to come and keep house for him."

"How long are you going to be away?"

"I don' know, but I'll get back as soon as I can. Goodbye now, Heironymous Geoff."

As he walked by Frank and George's cabin going back, he could hear them singing:

"You got to go to that lonesome valley,
You got to go there by yourself,
Oh nobody else can do it for you,
You got to go there all alone."

The next day, Geoff watched as Uncle Felix loaded Lulu and her children aboard his float-equipped Puss Moth airplane. After some ceremony, the comings-and-goings of airplanes at Poontuk are always an event, they were gone.

Chapter 15

The Weatherman's Badge

Canon Ford had laughingly and, to his wife only, often referred to Jerome Geoff as Saint Isaac, who was reputed to have started talking before he was born. Lately though, Mr. Ford had scolded himself for his epithet; because, when approached to conduct the local Scout Troop on a tour of the weather office and its facilities, Geoff had responded with enthusiasm. Indeed, with a hint or two from Mr. Ford, Geoff was happy to lecture the Scout and Cub organizations of the vagaries of weather, and taught them to read thermometers, barometers, hygrometers, and the theodolite scale.

"Mr. Ford tells me," Geoff declaimed one evening, "that in order to qualify for your weatherman's badge you must know the different cloud types. This is easy because meteorologists are very romantic. Take for example the cumulus cloud. That simply means 'heap' cloud. In the evening, when it's time for vespers, these clouds tend to lose their fluffiness and we call them 'cumulus vesperalis'. Now, when a cumulus cloud builds up and gets a fuzzy head on it we call that a 'cumulo-nimbus', a nimbus being just a fancy name for a halo. And when you get those big pouches hanging down below the thundercloud, you know, the big bulgey ones"- here, he made the classic "big boobs" gesture - "then that's called 'cumulo nimbus mammatus'."

"Jus' like Lulu," came a voice from the back.

It was duly noted in the "Notes of Interest" that the assistant weatherman at Fort Poontuk, who was also the paper's correspondent there, had been instrumental in qualifying a record number of Scouts for their weatherman's badge.

For Geoff, without Lulu, the nights were empty. He

would lie awake the night through listening to Edmonton radio stations coming but intermittently through the static. Alone and lost, his mood matching the popular songs: "I Can Dream, Can't I?" and "Room Full of Roses", he regretted his own lack of flexibility. He had never learned to play poker, and when he tried to join in the Monday and Thursday games, he was bewildered. Nobody wanted to show him the fundamentals, and he was at a loss to fathom the infinite complexities of Spit in the Ocean, Bicycle, Fiery Cross; High-Low Split with Jacks or Better to Open, sometimes five and sometimes seven card games. His books, writing and painting failed to engage him; he was always being diverted by the hope there would be that familiar tap on the window just above his bed, and he would find Lulu, her face aglow and her eyes sparkling, eager to join him. He was not at all troubled by what she might be doing in Norman Wells. It did not matter. So selfless, so generous was her nature, that Geoff found it mean-spirited to ascribe fidelity as well. He tried to convince himself that her generosity was but the license of a slut and he would conjure up the image of her writhing in another man's arms. But always she appeared as a cornucopia of sex, warmth and affection, pouring out with abundance but constantly being replenished; a kind of Earth Mother with the male involved remaining a shadowy insubstantial creature, a drone attending the queen.

The rumors about Salt were true. Every time Trent worked late at the station, Salt went visiting Jean. These visits had become almost a nightly routine, because Trent was working harder than ever to prepare for the approaching winter. Geoff wondered about the relationship between Salt and Jean Trent. It seemed impossible: That attractive woman sinning with that kinky little orphan, whose greatest joy as a child had been blowing up frogs with firecrackers. They couldn't be sleeping together! It must be strictly a hearts and flowers situation. Jean Trent was the type to bring home lost dogs and stray kittens, and poor Salt was one of these. Their public behavior offered no clues, though at the Friday night parties, Salt occasionally danced with her. He never danced before in his life. Geoff was amazed at his own reactions to the situations around him. While he could not feel the slightest jealousy about Lulu, he became irritated when he thought about Salt and Jean Trent together.

Residents of Poontuk didn't mention the affair among themselves, each assuming the other didn't know, and each, mindful of the keen dislike between Trent and Salt, fearful of saying anything that might even hint at it. The situation in the small community could have been intolerably delicate, but for Trent himself.

Trent was lost in his own world. He seemed to become drawn into an academic maze, where the more statistics became available, the wider became the field of investigation. This manifested itself by the appearance of a huge blackboard, which covered all of one wall in the weather office and which he covered with esoteric mathematical symbols and formulas. Geoff had checked out some of Trent's articles that had been published in the journals of learned societies. He thought he might get some glimpse of "the real Trent", but all he found were pages of mathematical notation, interspersed by language like: "If we assume that... then it follows that..." The man didn't think in language, he thought only in numbers, and his constant badgering of Geoff for more statistical information, summaries and abstracts was because he was trying to drown his error-prone humanity in the shining truth of numbers. That's why he couldn't relate to people, who were full of errors, and that's why his wife was stepping out on him; she wanted an erring, imperfect creature like herself, while Trent sought the perfection of numbers. Geoff smiled to himself: He had it all figured out.

Chapter 16

The District Meteorologist Visits

In the late summer season some of the men went hunting. Deer, moose and even bear meat were staples on Fort Poontuk's tables, because a kill provided far more meat than the hunter's family could use at once and refrigerating facilities in Poontuk were limited. At the single men's quarters, Scotty the cook's "pièce de résistance" was his roast grouse. He had an ample supply of the birds. The woods around Poontuk were full of the Fool Hens, which could be dispatched with a blow to the head. The birds tasted excessively gamey, a flaw eliminated when Scotty hung them until decay separated their bodies from their heads. "The goose hangs high!" Scotty would say, and go ahead with preparing the meal. Even the cooked meat smelled rotten, and took some getting used to. But after a time, the men grew to prefer it. Geoff was excited by the gustatory novelty and railed away about jugged hare, bird's nest soup, and the Chinese delicacy of eating alive, just-born mice dipped in honey.

The general wellbeing of the community was enhanced when at last the easterly winds veered into the prevailing west and the skies cleared. The sullen skies and ashen precipitation had had a depressing effect on everybody. With the appearance of the sun and the blue sky, the change to fresh, wholesome winds, the world was transformed. Nobody cared about the grey winter skulking on the horizon, or the significance of the boats toiling upstream to their winter berths to the south.

The skies had no sooner cleared than a twin-engine Electra aircraft came out of the receding mist, flashed over the community, and sped off for a landing at the airport. Bonnycastle rushed to the station. "Who is it?"

"It's the District Meteorologist," said Nichol. "There's something fishy about this whole deal, because I didn't get any flight plan on it."

"Think nothing of it," said Trent, walking in from his office. "It's a typical stunt for our Mr. L. Delance Babcock. He's throwing a surprise inspection. He probably left Fort Smith this morning and asked them to hold the flight plan."

"But, that's illegal" protested Nichol.

"That's the D. Met," said Trent.

When he and Bonnycastle reached the airport, three-quarters of an hour later, the pilot and co-pilot were waiting. They seemed to be amused about something.

Trent wanted to know, "What's up?"

They explained that the D. Met and his secretary, Mr. Bodnar, had elected to stay aboard the aircraft until transport to the community arrived. In the interval, Clarence Crunk had gone aboard the aircraft, and since then, they'd heard nothing but Crunk's voice, telling his audience about the state of his bowels. As an employee of the Department of Transport, Crunk seized the opportunity to petition the highest authorities for help with his peculiar problem.

"When I left the aircraft," said the pilot, "Crunk was saying that lately his turds have been hard as rocks. He has to strain a lot and he's worried about piles. So, he thinks that the D.O.T. should supply him with Preparation H. You should hear him, he's going into all kinds of detail."

"We know," chorused Trent and Bonnycastle.

Now Clarence Crunk was backing out of the aircraft. "So, if you'd just look into that," he was saying, "It would be of benefit to me and to the department which I serve because the state of the colon is of utmost importance. Worry and fret can cause trouble even more than faulty elimination. Speaking of that.."

"Yes, yes my good man," it was the voice of the D. Met. "We'll look into it, I assure you. Just let us get out. Mr.

Bodnar, take a note on that, will you."

"Yes, Mr. Babcock."

Crank walked by, looking flushed and triumphant. He didn't greet the others.

A foot appeared at the aircraft door. It extended outward, withdrew and then re-appeared, this time in the proper position to descend the ladder at the door. The foot was followed by a huge leg, wide buttocks in a shiny pair of navy blue trousers, and then, by the elephantine bulk of the D. Met in his entirety. He was assisted by Mr. Bodnar, at whom was directed a steady stream of minute instructions, till the unloading process was completed.

The D. Met looked about.

"Ah, Trent!" he exclaimed as they shook hands and made introductions all round, "Thank God you're here. That Crunk fellow seems to have an absolute obsession with his bowels. I never saw anything like it in my life. Well, let's get into town." He turned to the pilots. "You'll be staying out here with Crunk, eh?"

With that confirmed, he and Mr. Bodnar boarded the jeep for the trip into town, their suitcases balanced on their knees.

To cross the first stream, it was necessary to race the jeep on the downward slope for momentum to gain the further bank, a jolting procedure to which regular users of the road were accustomed. The newcomers were not.

As Bonnycastle crested the further bank, he was stopped by a frantic call for help. Mr. Bodnar had fallen out, and while the D. Met was still aboard, he'd lost his suitcase in the stream.

"Do you have to drive so furiously?" the D. Met snapped. Look what's happened!"

Bodnar had picked himself up from the shallow, muddy stream. He was soaked. Weeds clung to his clothes. He flung his suitcase back aboard the jeep.

"What about my suitcase? Get my suitcase, Mr. Bodnar!" shouted the D. Met, annoyed.

The clasps on the suitcase must have been loosened by the fall, for when Bodnar grasped the handle, the suitcase opened, and the D. Met's shirts, socks, ties and pyjamas tumbled into the stream.

"You idiot!" rumbled the D. Met as all rushed to rescue his haberdashery. In his efforts the D. Met got his feet wet. He started to sweat, attracting the flies.

"Let's get out of here," he growled. "And please, let's take the next stream crossing a little easier if you don't mind."

He applied copious amounts of insect repellent to his face, which, diluted by his sweat, entered his eyes.

"My God!" he cried. "My eyes! They may be severely impaired. I can't see! Stop the car!"

At the next stream the D. Met washed his face and dabbled his eyes, then reapplied the repellant only to his jowls. Flies attacked him steadily.

By the time the jeep trundled into Poontuk, the D. Met was in a high dudgeon and Mr. Bodnar was becoming anxious about him.

"Where do we sleep, where do we eat tonight?" asked the D. Met.

Geoff was to give up his room to the D. Met, and Bodnar would move into Salt's room. The regulars would sleep that night in bunks with Nepomuk Permaneder.

Introductions between the new arrivals and Geoff were cool and formal. When shown Geoff's room where he was to spend the night, the D. Met remarked:

"It smells strange."

Once settled, the D. Met toured the weather facilities, noting with alarm that work on the hydrogen shed was not as advanced as he had wished, and also that some of the new cold-weather equipment had not been installed. He felt that Trent should do something to tidy up his office. "After all,

Trent, cleanliness is next to Godliness. Mr. Bodnar, take a note."

All the while, he ate chocolate bars, which whetted his thirst. "Where can one buy pop in this down?" he inquired of Scotty, the cook.

"Well, I can't remember the last time I saw pop. But wait a minute." Scotty disappeared and returned with about five almost-empty bottles of Scotch, rye, rum, vodka and some liqueur. "Sorry, that's all there is, but it's between plane days."

"I don't drink whiskey!" thundered the D. Met, shocked. "Well now, hold on," said Scotty as he went down into the cellar and fetched up a half-dozen beer bottles. "It's apricot wine. We had a whole bowl go bad on us, so we just tossed in some yeast, got it cooking, bottled it with some sugar, and it's not bad. Here, try it yourself.."

"I never indulge in spirituous liquors!" said the D. Met.

It was time for supper, and Scotty had prepared his specialty, roast grouse.

Geoff and Salt fell to their meal with gusto. The D. Met and Bodnar immediately the fare was placed under their noses, recoiled in horror.

"But this meat is rotten!" declared the D. Met.

"That's right," said Geoff. "The meat is rotten. But it's the only way you can eat it. Gets rid of the gamey taste. Try it. It's a real gourmet's dish."

The D. Met blanched. Beads of sweat started from his brow. "I don't feel too well, he said. "Perhaps I'd better lie down."

Later, he contented himself with a cup of Postum. It didn't have much flavor, and Scotty explained the Postum had been on the shelves for at least five years.

That evening, the men of the town assembled in the common room for poker and drinking, much to the disgust of the D. Met. He and Mr. Bodnar sat in one corner of the room reading month-old magazines, unable even to hear the record player for the spirited comments of the poker-players.

"C'mon, Mr. Babcock," Sergeant Sitter invited him for the fifth time. "Come and sit in here and find out the everlasting mysteries of five-card."

"Thank you, no. I'll just sit here and read."

"Ah, c'mon, you can do that anywhere."

The D. Met deigned not to answer.

"Hey, Mr. Babcock," Nichol said. "Have you tried Scotty's "specialité de la maison", the Grouse?"

"I think I'll go to bed now", said the D. Met, disappearing into his assigned room.

Mr. Bodnar waited a decent interval and then said to Sitter, "About that offer for over proof rum. You can't buy it in Alberta, you know. I'd like to try it."

"By all means, Mr. Bodnar," replied Sitter. "Hey, I can't go around calling you Mister all the time. What do they call you when they want you in a hurry?"

"My first name is Harold."

"Okay, Harold" said Sitter. "Come with me."

In the kitchen, Sitter prepared hot buttered rum. Bodnar drank it, owned that it was marvelous, and asked if the might have another.

"As a matter of fact," he told Sitter in a confidential mien, "this is the first bloody nice thing that's happened to me since we started the trip. Traveling with that man," Bodnar here gestured to indicate a big stomach, "is no holiday."

"Well, finish that one off, Harold," said Sitter. "I'm sure we can find enough stuff to make you another. Chimo!"

Later, Nepomuk Permaneder joined the party in the kitchen, and when Sitter went back to join the poker game, Permaneder and Bodnar began a tete-a-tete. Later, they both went out.

For the D. Met, the night was a trial. Just when he

thought the poker playing and partying was about to subside, it would flare anew. Loud shouting from the common room roused him continually. There was a faint glow on the horizon when he at last fell into a wretched sleep.

He was jolted awake; this time more forcefully than in the times previous. For somebody was moving stealthily about the room.

"Who is it?" he muttered, barely audibly.

Whoever it was weaved to and fro and crashed into the wardrobe.

"Who is it?" stronger this time, and with unfamiliar hands, the D. Met sought the switch for the light.

The light came on. Standing at the foot of the bed with clothes in disarray, and a stunned expression, was Harold Bodnar.

"Jesus!" said Bodnar vehemently. "I come to the wrong room. Sorry about that."

"Mr. Bodnar," said the D. Met, rising from his bed. "I believe you're drunk..and worse."

Bodnar's face was covered with lipstick.

"Yeah," said Bodnar. "I'm drunk and I been out on the town." He stuffed his hands in his pockets and swayed on fixed feet. "Wow! Did I ever have a good time! Gotta smoke?"

"Mr. Bodnar," said the D. Met. "It's late and I suggest you go to bed. I would remind you, Mr. Bodnar, that we're touring the north to inspect weather offices, not to indulge in drunken debauchery at every turn. I would remind you, too, that your position as my secretary is not all that firm. Do you understand? It would behoove you, therefore, to mind your P's and Q's. I've had a very trying time so far on this trip, and your behavior isn't helping. This is something I'll remember next time I consider your replacement. Good night, Mr. Bodnar."

"I said, good night, Mr. Bodnar"

"Up your gee-gee with a wire brush, you Mormon bastard!" shouted Bodnar.

Bodnar wove his way out and could be heard bumping into the table, thumping against a chair and crashing into an ashtray.

The D. Met buried his head in his hands. "Oh God," he thought. "I should leave this God-forsaken place right now." He would have, had not the thought of the trip over the treacherous road in the dim light of dawn given him pause. He went to the kitchen for a glass of water, contemplated his fate, used the bathroom, and returned.

He had some trouble relaxing enough for sleep, but again he was jarred awake. Again, somebody was moving about in the room.

He rose, now in a towering rage. He flung the bedclothes from him and crashed his feet to the floor. "Now! I'm going to put a stop to this once and for all!" he roared.

Somebody sniggered, and the D. Met switched on the light. At the foot of the bed stood a woman. That's the first immediate impression the D. Met had, a woman was standing there with the hem of her voluminous caftan pulled up to her bosom. In the rush of impressions that impinged on his battered sensibilities, he was aware of long, naked legs and dark pubic patch, revealed for just a moment before the curtain was rung down.

The D. Met's expression changed from outrage to horror. He drew the sheets up to his chin and cringed in the corner of the bed.

"What to you want?" he spluttered. He thought he might faint.

The intruder's face burst into a sun-flash of mischief. She said nothing, just grinned at him.

Near panic, the D. Met flung himself against the wall. Then, he discovered the window was open and, with dexterity surprising for his bulk, he twisted around and launched his upper body out the window.

Lulu in reaching out had grasped his pyjama trousers, and, as the big man sailed out, the bottoms came off in her hands.

"Help! Help! For God's sake, won't somebody help!" cried the D. Met.

Parnell came rushing from the station. Unable to make out quite what was happening in the dim, early-morning light, he switched on the yard lamp. The D. Met was just rounding the far corner of the building, running as if his life depended on it, his buttocks like puffed-up bread dough, while Lulu, her caftan held high in one hand and flourishing the pyjama bottoms with the other, chased after him.

"Stop! Stop! You forgot something!" she called, breaking down in a fit of laughter.

The noise awakened the Single Men's Quarters. Harold Bodnar, on looking out, could scarcely believe his eyes. The running couple had now circled the building, and to Bodnar, it appeared the D. Met was chasing Lulu, and he without his pyjama bottoms!

"My God!" cried Bodnar. With that, he flung himself back to bed.

A new player entered the scene. Sprinting down the road could be seen the lean, wiry figure of Uncle Felix. Lulu spotted Felix at once and caught up with and pushed the D. Met.

"Run!" she cried urgently. "Run quick down the road!"

"Stop!" commanded Uncle Felix brandishing a hunting knife.

Instantly, Parnell disappeared into the station.

Felix was bearing down on the D. Met., who, seeing the savage rage on his pursuer's face fetched from within himself new energies. He turned and fled. Lulu meantime leaped on Felix's back, jammed the pyjama bottoms over his head, and at the same time, tried to wrest the knife from his hand.

Down they went, grappling about in the dust of the road, screaming and shouting, arms and legs flailing. Felix at last managed to push her aside, sprang to his feet, and pulled off the pyjamas, flinging them over the river bank. Then he sped off after the D. Met.

Then came another pyjama-clad figure, sprinting at top speed, from the same general direction whence Felix had come. It was Button, shouting as loudly as he could.

The shouting startled Felix, who stopped for an instant. That provided Button with the opportunity to crash into Felix with a flying tackle that drove him thudding to the ground.

Felix writhed about, retching and gasping, the wind knocked out of him.

"Get out of here," said Button to Lulu. "Quick!" Button was panting hard.

By now, some others, Bonnycastle, Geoff, Permaneder and Salt were gathering.

Button looked down at Felix: "I think at last we may have something to pin on this character," he said. "Assault with a deadly weapon with intent. That ought to hold up in court. You know, this guy is also wanted to answer a few questions because of a mysterious disappearance up on Bear Lake." He laughed. "And you guys know us Royal Canadian Mounted Cops, once we get going after somebody..." Button reached down and dragged the unprotesting Felix to his feet. "Come with me. I must warn you; you are now under arrest and anything you say from now on may be taken down and.."

The warning continued as Button pulled the foot-dragging prisoner by the nape of the neck.

The D. Met joined the gathering. In his confusion and outrage he seemed demented, standing there before them, his face purple, gasping for breath, and without his pyjama bottoms. He stood and said nothing, embarrassing the others. They could think of nothing to say.

Finally, Bonnycastle cleared his throat. "Will you be staying another day, Mr. Babcock?"

"Huh?" said the D. Met, who seemed to be emerging as from a dream.

Bonnycastle smiled politely. "I was wondering if you and Mr. Bodnar would be staying for another day?"

"Well now, I don't know," said the D. Met. He stared about distractedly in the grey light. His sparse hair straggled down over his eyes. "What was that you said?"

Bonnycastle coughed. He wished the visitor would leave and get dressed. What if some women, or Mr. Ford, were to come along.

"Are you going to stay?"

"What?" The light was coming back into the D. Met's eyes. "Stay in this Hell of Lucifer? Not on your life. Gentlemen, I've had it. And believe you me; you've had it, too! Don't ever think for one moment I'll let this go by without word to the proper authorities. I'll never forget what's happened here. Do you hear me? Never!"

"Greeted at the airport by a monomaniac, who can talk about nothing but his bowels and his piles; almost killed on our way in here; our baggage dropped in a stream full of muck and weeds, our clothes ruined; offered rotten meat to eat and nothing but whiskey to drink. I was kept up all night by drinking and gambling ruffians. My secretary, debauched by strong drink and loose women. My very person set upon by a lascivious woman, who actually attacked me. Then, on top of all this, threatened by a man with a knife! You ask me if I'm going to stay?" He was on the verge of hysteria. "The answer is, no! Not one minute more. Get the jeep! I don't care anymore. I'll not stay in this place one minute longer!" With that, the D. Met strode purposefully toward the building. "Mr. Bodnar! Mr. Bodnar!" he called.

Then he looked down, suddenly aware of his bottomless condition. His mouth dropped open and he turned to face the others. They in turn stared dumbly at him for a moment, then, averted their gazes, mumbling apologies and clearing throats. The D. Met with a jerk, covered his private parts, and, in a bent-knee, stooped-over posture, scurried to the quarters. Within, he could be heard bawling: "Mr. Bodnar! Mr. Bodnar! We're leaving!"

Lulu told Geoff all about her sojourn with Uncle Felix that very evening. Felix's relations with his niece, after several days, were not so avuncular as avaricious and he was after her for a more intimate relationship. Lulu, despite Felix's argument that they were not really uncle and niece, was revolted. Blood relation or not, it was not right. There'd been a fight in which Felix blackened her eye, and might have done worse had not Lulu's children started crying. So while Felix was away at work, Lulu sized on an opportunity to get aboard one of the southbound boats, bringing her children with her. Felix was away for two days, and when he returned and found her gone, immediately jumped into his airplane and came after her.

Her time with Felix, Geoff thought, should have filled her with overpowering fear for her life or the lives of her children, privy as she was to the certain knowledge that he had killed a man. While drunk, he had told Lulu that he had strangled his partner, who owned a fifty-percent share in the Caterpillar tractor. The partner wanted to take the machine to Yellowknife, the metropolis of the north, with its cocktail bars, women, gambling and easy access to the Outside, to say nothing of the construction boom the town was enjoying. But Felix saw there was a fortune to be made close at hand. The entire community of Aklavik, on the Mackenzie delta, was to be moved to higher ground to form the new town of Inuvik. Their 'dozer would be working night and day once the big moving job got underway. It was a government job, and Felix knew that in projects like this, the government spends lavishly. They'd have a guaranteed source of income. The partner didn't see it that way, and on more than one occasion, he and Felix were seen arguing violently. One day, the partner vanished. Felix said he didn't know what had happened to him. It was thought the partner had left the country. But one day, his body surfaced on Great Bear Lake. It was the merest chance the body was found at all considering the immensity of the lake, the frequent storms and winter's preparing to seal it over.

But Lulu understood. "It was God comin' down in his wrath against Uncle Felix for all da bad tins he done. Now he's goin' to jail in Fort Smit."

Weeks later, word also came forth that the D. Met had resigned. Those who took the Edmonton newspapers learned that: "L. Delance Babcock, who was chiefly responsible for setting up the network of northern weather stations, will step down, effective the end of October. Mr. Babcock, who is fifty-nine, takes early retirement following a harrowing tour of Canada's frozen north." Both newspapers carried pictures of the man being honored at various functions. Babcock was shown in the stark pointillism of rotogravure, staring dazedly at the camera, as some official from the Department of Transport shook his hand and presented him with a certificate of merit. A successor to Mr. Babcock had yet to be named.

It snowed again in Fort Poontuk, and this time, the snow stayed. Winter had struck a blow and the summer season, unable to marshal any counter attack, could be seen yielding the field. The sun blanched, and spent less time each day above the horizon. The wind bespoke an even worse time to come. It was during one of the howling northerlies that the cabin used as a school by Canon Ford took fire and burned to the ground. Nobody was hurt and the cause was attributed to an overheated, pot-bellied stove. Fires of any extent in Poontuk always meant total destruction. The settlement was without fire-fighting resources. Canon Ford's classes were moved to Harry Crum's Hotel.

The play's progress suffered the usual vicissitudes of amateur productions. The director, Mr. Ford, could seldom get all the cast together at once; one or two always had a previous engagement. It was poker night, or Lux radio theatre night, or the director himself had a Cub and Scout committee meeting. Jerry Geoff, the great discourser on the Method and the deeper philosophy of dramaturge, usually arrived dead tired, without a spark of energy for the play.

"Really Jerry," said Ford. "If there's one thing this play needs, it's theatrical energy. I must ask that you put more attack into your part. After all, if you don't believe it, your audience won't either."

Nor could Constable Button lose himself in his role. He played the Convict, and at one point, had to confront the Bishop (Mr. Ford) with these lines: "Humph! I'll risk it. But mind! Play me false and as sure as there are devils in Hell, I'll drive my knife through your heart. I have nothing to lose."

Button never got to the last sentence. The speech conjured up the image of Mr. Babcock fleeing without his pyjama bottoms with knife-wielding Uncle Felix in hot pursuit, and Button would collapse into laughter before the end of his speech.

"Please, Kenneth," scolded Ford. "You've got to take this more seriously. Concentrate on what you're saying. Consider your predicament before the Bishop. Acting is concentration. Concentrate and you'll get the line. You'll become that character."

"Mrs. Prout, who'd played the Bishop's shrewish sister and housekeeper was not so diplomatic. "'ere," she said. "Oi got better things ta do than to muck about wi' you lot, if you won't pie attention. Oi don't 'ave no trouble wif my part."

Then, one evening the cast stepped from Harry Crum's hotel to find it surprisingly dark, as if hours had suddenly been cut from the day, a cold, sullen wind was abroad, and glinting ice crystals filled the air. Winter had come. As they walked home they could feel the cold air stealing into every breach in their clothing and they knew it was time for the storm-cuffed ski pants, time for parkas, mitts and mukluks, time to get into the winter cocoon.

Similarly, the environs around Poontuk became cloaked. Throughout the summer, a mountain was visible far to the east. The weathermen used it as a popular if unreliable forecaster, for it seemed as long as the mountain flaunted a tiny white cloud at its summit the weather remained sunny. When the cloud disappeared, the weather deteriorated. Now the entire mountain had disappeared in the thickening grey slate of winter's horizon.

As they passed Frank and George's cabin, Geoff and Lulu stopped to listen:

"In the land of the pale blue snow

Where it's ninety-nine below,

And the polar bear goes wanderin' o'er the plain,

In the shadow of the pole,

I will clasp her to my soul,

We'll be happy when the ice-worms nest again."

Lulu said: "I tink the winter time is best for love-makin', 'cause it's so dark mos' of da time and you don' have to do so much slippin' around."

She looked around and then grinned at him. She took his hand and guided it down the back of her slacks till it rested on her buttocks. "See! Dey're so cold. C'mon and you can warm dem up for me."

Afterward, Geoff confessed to her that when it came to the art of coition, Lulu was a PhD and worthy of the Governor-General's gold Medal. "I'm not kidding," he told her, and he watched with surprise as she blushed, as she usually did, when he flattered her. "They ought to give you a knight-hood. I can see it now: 'Arise Dame Hannah-Maria Burns, arise. At least get off your back long enough to accept the accolade.'"

"I don know what you're talkin' 'bout. I don' spend all my time on my back. Dat's not a nice thin' to say."

"I didn't mean anything by it, I was just making fun, that's all."

"Sometimes", she said, looking at him very seriously, "Sometimes I don' like your way of havin' fun. 'Bout being on my back all the time. D'you thin' I'm like a whore. Izzat what you mean, Heironymous Geoff?"

"No, that's not it at all, I only..."

"I tin' I'll go home early tonight. No, don' you get up, I'll go home by mysel'"

"Will I see you tomorrow night?"

"Maybe yes, maybe no. We'll see."

She did not come the next night, nor the next.

Chapter 17

Armistice Day

Bonnycastle had a hard time convincing Canon Ford year after year that he meant it when he said his men would not parade on Armistice Day with the Scouts and Cubs.

"I haven't got enough men", argued Bonnycastle. "It would just look ridiculous."

But he did agree to urge all off-duty Signalmen to put up their "gongs" - as they called their wartime medals and decorations - and attend the Armistice Service at the Church.

Prior to the November 11th Service, the men gathered for hot rums in the common room. They were shaved and shorn, and in their freshly pressed uniforms with gongs flashing and tinkling, looked quite smart. Button was splendid in his scarlet tunic, blue breeks with the distinctive gold stripe, and high brown boots. While they wouldn't march with the youngsters, the men felt no compunction in getting together for a drink and then going to church in a body. They would all come back afterward and finish off what was left. So, even though it was twenty degrees below zero Fahrenheit outside and threatening snow, spirits were high in the common room. The Signal Corps, the Army Service Corps and the RCMP would be represented at the service. Nobody had asked former pilot Trent to join the parade, and he hadn't volunteered to do so. For the soldiers in the common room, such behavior was to be expected of "Fly Boys".

Drinks were bottoms-ed up and the party prepared to dash to the church. They would not wear greatcoats, as this would only cover up their ribbons and gongs, and gloves were the only concession to the weather. They were about to leave when a voice bellowed: "Vait for me!" It was Nepomuk

Permaneder.

Permaneder marched into the common room and stood at attention so they could all get a good look. Nepomuk was attired in the green-grey tunic and cap of a private in the German Army. On his chest was pinned his Iron Cross.

The chattering troop of men fell silent. Appleyard, the only member of the group to be decorated, reacted strongly to the appearance of the enemy uniform. "What you doin'?"

"I vant go to de service," said Nepomuk.

Appleyard came forward. "Yeh, but you can't.. it ain't right.." he muttered, unable to find words.

Nepomuk had no such trouble. His military posture was dropped as he spoke: "Now, listen to me. Everybody knows za var is crazy. One time you shot Germans and Japanese, next time, maybe ve all gang up and shoot da goddamn Russians. Who knows? Only ze bosses. One time ze yankees shoot ze English and ze French shoot everybody, but vat ze hell! Ze only guys get hurt are guys like you and me. Yesterday, ve fight, today ve friends. You vant remember your friends today. So do I. So vat de Hell! Haf a drink!" He waved his bottle of scotch.

Appleyard was relieved. He smiled and said: "C'mon, I wonder what Mr. Ford will say about this!"

The Canon was indeed surprised, but pleased. He smiled.

"Ladies and Gentlemen, boys and girls of the congregation, this morning, we have something very unusual here. And I for one think it's a very good thing. Because I think it points out that, no matter what the color of a man's skin, or his nationality, or the uniform he wears, we are all God's children. While wars go on there's but little we can do; it's out of our hands. But when the war is over, we should forget and we should forgive. As Christ told Peter: 'I do not say to you to forgive seven times, but seventy times seven.'"

Canon Ford was inspired by the significance of the German uniform to such an extent that he set aside his usual sermon about remembering and honoring the fallen of the two World Wars for their sacrifice in defense of freedom everywhere; and extemporized on the need for love around the world. For this he drew with practiced ease from Corinthians: "Though I speak with the tongues of men and of angels and have not charity..."

The sermon, considering the occasion, was so entirely different that the entire congregation stayed awake the whole time. When it came time to stand and shake hands at the church door, the Canon was aglow.

"Mr. Permaneder," he said. "It took courage to do what you did. Frankly, I was shocked, and then I was glad. I think Fort Poontuk can now claim the distinction of being the only place in Canada to hold services not only for both World Wars, but for both sides."

Ford joined the men for a drink afterward at the single men's common room. His presence kept the party's tenor low and conservative, but gave the men a self-righteous Sunday School feeling; at least for awhile.

News of the unusual Armistice Day service at Fort Poontuk was spread abroad by the "Notes of Interest". Within a few weeks, Bonnycastle had received a number of letters from ex-servicemen all across the north, unanimously condemning the affair. "Two years ago, we were shooting the bastards," one writer stated in his letter. "Now you're honoring them in church. Where will all this lead?" Bonnycastle received a letter on official stationery from the Secretary of the Fort Smith Branch of the Canadian Legion, saying that the Armistice Day service in Fort Poontuk had been carried out in "very questionable" circumstances. A full report was requested. But then another letter, this one signed by the President of the Fort Smith Legion Branch arrived, saying the first letter should be ignored as the

Secretary had written it without the consent or guidance of the general membership of the Branch.

Canon Ford didn't know what to expect. Would he be disciplined for his remarks? What had he said, really. He had been suddenly inspired and had simply run off at the mouth. Thank heaven there'd been no professional reporter there. He could see the headlines: "Anglican Minister Lauds German Soldier at Armistice Day Ceremony!" or "German soldier singled out for special praise by Anglican Minister at Armistice Day Parade." He would have been defrocked!

The affair was soon forgotten, never reaching the notice of the bigger newspapers.

If Nepomuk Permaneder's daring enterprise had engendered a spontaneous outburst of brotherly love, the altruism was brought to full flower during the party afterward, and more especially after the Canon had taken his leave. It was between plane days, but somehow more and more liquor kept turning up. It was like one of the Post Armistice Day service parties on the Outside; strictly a man's affair, lots of drinking, lots of singing of the old war-time songs. Even Frank and George showed up. They hadn't done so before as they couldn't be bothered with 'these young fellers who can't hold their booze' but with the singing going on hour after hour, their resistance was overcome. They brought some booze with them. Somehow "Jock" Robinson managed to sneak away from Mrs. Prout and he joined the party, bringing his pipes with him. The singing of war-time songs, depression songs, and a spate of "tent-meeting revival" songs from Frank and George kept the party going all night. A minor crisis developed when Signalman Nichol, who was to relieve Salt on the evening shift, passed out while singing: "I want a beer, just like the beer that pickled dear old Dad." Finally Sergeant Sitter himself had to fill in while they tried to bring Nichol around.

It was dawn the next day before the riotous singing, sentimental bag-pipe blaring, smoky and drunken affair at last wound down.

Jerome Geoff awoke with at start. Where was he? He looked about, but in his drink befogged state and the dim light, he could discern nothing. He groped about and his hand fell upon a firm, ample breast. Lulu! She turned sleepily to push her breast harder against his hand, which he withdrew.

She moaned: "Don' do dat."

"Lulu, are you awake?"

"No"

"How the hell did I get down here last night? I don't even remember coming here."

"You said you came to apologize to me for the terrible tins you said."

"I did?"

"Yes, Heironymous Geoff, and I accepted your apologies." She suddenly giggled. "You were a perfect gentleman 'bout it. Hey! You even wore a necktie. Firs' time I seen one of those tins for years!"

"Oh."

"Den you came to bed wif me."

"Oh, No!" Geoff suddenly felt a wave of nausea brought on by self-loathing as much as the booze.

She kissed him primly on the mouth and said: "Don' worry, da kids was asleep, and besides, you couldn't get it up!"

"Oh no!" another wave of nausea.

She was pushing herself on him, drawing the hard nipples of her breasts up and down his back. The fingers of her left hand went marching slowly around his waist and grabbed his penis. She whispered in his ear, "It's early. Let's do it"

It was impossible. Geoff tried a rueful little laugh, and

then realized how sick he was. Poised on the razor's edge between nausea and the catharsis of vomiting; afraid to move, afraid to breathe.

Her hand moved gently over his testicles. His mouth filled with saliva and his stomach contracted. He clamped a hand to his mouth and tried to get out of bed. It was too late.

In the after-spasms of coughing, hiccupping and retching, he appeared a ruined man. His face was the palest green, his eyes, blood red, lips purple, and tears coursed down his cheeks.

She ran and fetched a bucket and started to clean up. Geoff said: "Hey, let me do that, you shouldn't have to do that." But he knew he was just being polite.

She looked at him, amused and sympathetic at his condition. "It's all right, Heironymous Geoff. I don' mind. It was so nice of you to come and see me las' night."

"Oh no, Lulu. You shouldn't say that." A dying man can unburden his soul with honesty and candor. "I got pretty drunk last night, and the only reason I came down here was to..."

"So you could apologize," she said, fixing her eyes on his.

After a moment, he said, "Yeah, I guess that's right."

The baby at the foot of the bed started to stir. Geoff could hear the crone's bedsprings twang as she moved about. The cabin was coming to life. Geoff felt like an interloper.

"I'd better be going," he said. "I've got work to do."

"I come and see you tonight," she said.

It was cold outside. The sky was dark and scowling, pressing low so as to isolate Fort Poontuk from the rest of the world. Now and then a furtive ice crystal fell, the wind was restless and swirling, the usually silent river gulped mysteriously, and Geoff was sickeningly reminded of Dante's Third Circle in Hell, the one reserved for the gluttonous, with its unending snow, icy wind and dark water.

More torments awaited him.

In the hilarity of yesterday's Armistice Party, a prime fiat of the north had been forgotten: Don't throw cigarettes in the toilet. Excrement was processed efficiently by the bacteria in the septic tank - even when it was sixty below - but these bacteria couldn't tolerate tobacco.

Immediately he entered the door, Geoff knew the truth. His nostrils were assailed with the mephitic stench, and, summoning a great effort of will, he inspected the dugout basement, were all their food was stored. It was a horror, ankle deep in urine and turds.

Frank and George cleaned it up, and with astonishing cheerfulness. They took some sort of pride in doing work which the others would have found impossible, and reminded Geoff of the first year medical students at the University of Alberta, who used to eat their sandwiches at lunchtime in the "stiff lab", the room filled with dismembered cadavers, to show how tough they were. With Frank and George, it was the same species of bravura (and also for fifty dollars and found) as they sang at their work:

"He lifted me up, yes up!
Up from the mirey clay.
He lifted me up, yes up!
To walk the narrow way.
He lifted me up, yes up!
I'm bound for Heaven's shore,
He lifted me up, yes up!
To live for evermore!"

For Geoff and the others, the day warranted a fast, and they spent their time gloomily contemplating the river. The burden of ice was increasing, and the bump and crush of one ice block upon another began a long crescendo, which would not climax until the freeze-up came.

Chapter 18

Permaneder Completes the Hydrogen Shed

She was the most wonderful woman he had ever known. She was good looking, and her figure, in a sturdy, matronly manner, was good to look at too. But it was what was inside, the love and understanding that glowed in her brown eyes that captivated Salt. Jean Trent had caught him that night, standing as he was at her bedroom window in the dark. She didn't scream or make a scene, when she could have called him every dirty name she would lay her tongue to. He'd been caught red-handed, a dirty, rotten peeping Tom! Salt would never forget that pang of pain, horror, and disgust so poignant, he wanted the earth to open and swallow him, when her soft voice came out of the dark, "Why Paul, is that you?" As if what he were doing was the most natural thing in the world. She said: "You can't stand out there in the cold, come on in. Let's have some coffee."

From the start, she never made mention of that encounter. At first it puzzled Salt, and he was uneasy in her presence, as if she were playing some game and he were the unwitting cat's paw. But this was not the case at all. After they'd gone in she said, again, as if it were almost a routine matter, they should sit in the front room. "Cy always comes in the back door and this way you can go out the front. We're lucky. Most of the cabins in this town only have the one door." No mention, not at first anyway, of the enmity between him and her husband.

She was patient, she was kind, and she genuinely understood his need to tell of his childhood, about the institutions and foster homes, the routine cruelties and put-downs, when nobody really cared for or about him, except for a show of affection and concern whenever the inspectors came around.

He wanted to get it all out. About the strange, unshaven old man, smelling of whiskey, who was always pinching and squeezing him at the nursing mission. That all ended when the man's balls swelled so badly he couldn't walk and he was taken away. The women talked about him in whispers and shut up altogether when Paul was within earshot. The summer camp, when for three days in a row, he stood up and was introduced to different groups of visiting businessmen as one of the "underprivileged" their money had helped bring to camp.

Parcels came at Christmastime and Easter. Salt told Jean that he thought life was simply a series of hand-outs, a dry crust of bread now and then to keep you from one bleak day to the next until you ended up like that dirty old man with the swollen balls and had to be "put away" with corkscrew germs gouging out your brains.

But it all changed on a day in 1939. The King and Queen were visiting, and Salt, along with thousands of other youngsters, was marched down early in the morning to a position on the royal parade route. They were issued flags, the Union Jack and the Red Ensign, and later on that morning got free milk and doughnuts. Then the great moment came with the royal couple, King George and Queen Elizabeth, riding by in their magnificent car. A whole new world was opened up to Salt. There was something outside the chipped and peeling walls of the nursing missions, the worn sofas of the foster homes, the miserable women and ratty old men. A world marvelous beyond his dreams, and made up of brass bands, their instruments blazing in the morning light, scarlet tunics and busbies, Mounties, flags, and then Their Majesties, fairy-book figures come to life, turning and smiling and waving at him. Then came the war, and for King and Country, Salt couldn't join up fast enough. He lied about his age to get in.

Jean said: "You served with a reconnaissance unit, Paul.

But wasn't that dangerous? I mean, from what I've heard the others say, joining a recon' patrol was like being a tail-gunner in the Air Force. A good way to keep from growing old."

"That's right," replied Salt proudly. "I was in the Fifty-ninth Recon Squadron. The main duties of the recon' patrol were to go out and make contact with the enemy. It was our job to find out where the enemy was, how many of them, and what kind of equipment they had, the position and strength of the enemy."

He was so proud, he went on and on, and her attention never flagged. Until she said: "Paul, it's almost midnight. Cy's going to be home any minute now. He's very punctual you know, so off you get,"

"All right. I gotta work tomorrow night, but if it's okay with you, I'll come over for coffee, y'know, if things work out all right the evening after. That's if it's all right with you..Jean."

She smiled warmly and said: "I wonder what people are thinking?" And when no answer came, "Goodnight, Paul."

Paul Salt, walking home, was oblivious of the bitter cold of the Arctic winter. He felt calm with a new sense of self-respect and respect for others. He thought back at some of the cruel things he'd said and done. He shuddered. But there was hope that he could now change his ways, and if he could never heal the wounds of those he'd offended in years past, he could compensate in the future. He was surprised at his day-to-day attitude to those around him. He began to see things in people he'd not noticed or appreciated before. Maybe you could teach an old dog new tricks, maybe he could change his ways completely and become a new person. Hell, some nights when he sat there with Jean he could even feel half-way sorry for Trent, who, for all his education and learning, didn't know what life was all about, while he, Paul Salt, was at least beginning to find out. The secret is in having someone who loves and understands you. With

Trent, Jean did not make this connection, but with him, she did. As he walked home he allowed himself to slip into his favorite fantasy: Trent gone, dead, left forever, anyway not around and the moment when duffel bag in hand, he would enter the front door of Jean's home and announce that he'd come to stay forever. She would come forward, nestle in his arms and offer her mouth to be kissed, slowly opening her lips. He dashed the vision from his mind. It was stupid to even think of such a thing. What the hell did he want? Jean Trent was just a very good person feeling sorry for a poor orphan boy and it was just stupid for him to think she felt anything else. She was his sounding board. She would sit and listen to him for hours - he wondered why she didn't fall asleep - while he went on and on. It was a one-way street, with him doing all the talking and her the listening. Not exactly the knight in shining armor come to carry off the princess, while the scarlet coated bandsmen played and the King and Queen waved encouragement and best wishes. He didn't stand a change for a lasting relationship with Jean. When Trent had finished his work - possibly by this winter - she'd be gone, and he'd be alone again. And yet... and yet...

It woke people up in the middle of the night. Not an explosion, nor anything calamitous: But, a sound, an ambience all in Fort Poontuk had learned to live with, stopped. The river was frozen. For weeks, for months prior to that December the eighth, the river had been carrying ever increasing squadrons of ice pans, until they were in such numbers that they obliterated completely the water that carried them; going by like a vast navy of ghostly ships in all shapes and sizes, bumping and thumping and crashing and groaning day and night; moving slower and slower until they all stopped. Silence descended on Poontuk like a cloak.

Trent noted it in the weather office's daily report. "River froze over at 1:00 PM, December 8th 1947. This is about one week earlier than normal." And, he gloomily confessed, probably meant that he'd not be getting any Chinook-like winds this winter. The meteors were conspiring against him. Where he wanted dominance on the weather map of the warm Aleutian low pressure system, he got instead dominance from a series of high pressure systems which moved from the cold pole of the world in Siberia. These latter systems were inordinately cold - reports from Siberia showed Verkhoyansk threatening to go to ninety degrees below zero - and while there would be some modification when these systems reached Canada, they would not warm up much. It was doubtful that Trent would be permitted to stay another season in quest of his elusive wind, which, to hard-nosed administrators on the Outside who held the purse strings, were not all that important.

Two days after the freeze up, two things happened: the temperature, despite Trent's prediction of fairly mild weather, went down to 45 below, and Nepomuk announced that the hydrogen shed was finished, at least to the point that the weathermen could use it to generate the gas.

It was a dangerous business. The cylinders in which the gas was generated were forever blowing up – as had happened just last winter down at Fort Smith - but it was universally agreed this was because weathermen were always trying to generate too much gas at once, so they could skip the chore a couple of times. The cylinder was tilted at a forty-five degree angle, and caustic soda and water sloshed down. Next, aluminum filings were tapped in, these adhering to the top of the cylinder until it was swung to the upright position. Then the aluminum particles fell into the caustic solution and the chemical reaction yielding hydrogen ensued. The reaction was so violent that the heat produced was enough to warm the shed during the coldest weather, and the cylinder remained too hot to touch for an hour.

So the measurement of Fort Poontuk's upper air currents got underway again. In the cold weather, the balloons went straight up, like a reverse plumb line, to twenty thousand feet. The cold had so vitiated the atmosphere it seemed lifeless, unable to move.

Canon Ford came to see Trent.

"Is it going to warm up, do you think, in the next couple of days?"

"No. The pressures are going up all over the map. Don't think there'll be any break in the weather," said Trent. Why do you ask? I thought you'd be getting used to it by now."

"Oh no, it's not me, " said Ford. "It's the Christmas Concert. I thought that if warmer weather was coming we could postpone it a couple of days and maybe get a better crowd out, but if its not going to change we might as well go ahead as planned."

Chapter 19

Christmas Concert

C hristmas Concert night was bitterly cold. Mrs. Ford, as mistress of ceremonies, didn't bother to remove her ski-pants from under, or her cardigan from over her filmy chiffon gown. The other women took their cue from her and remained similarly dressed. Most even kept their parkas on, but as the hall at Harry Crum's hotel filled, it warmed up and these came off. Canon Ford was ecstatic. Running back and forth, seeing to the selling of coffee and cookies, checking with the backstage help, going over the program of events for the one-hundredth time, he wore a smile of genuine satisfaction and felt the glad heart of any impresario when he plays to a full house. And he felt that the time and travail in sledding the piano from his house to the hall was well worth the effort.

"There must be one hundred fifty at least," he enthused. "Everybody's here, most of the whites, all the natives, either out front or performing. Oh, it'll be a grand evening!"

Finally, the house lights went out and Fraser Bourque, Poontuk's only King's Scout Candidate, resplendent in his badges and other accoutrements, came forward to announce that the Annual Christmas Concert was about to begin. Then he blew a ragged fanfare on his trumpet and rushed off the stage, forgetting to announce the Mistress of Ceremonies.

The crowd cheered, and a rum wave, almost palpable in its richness, burst on the stage, as Mrs. Ford came on.

To say that the crowd was warm and enthusiastic, was to say the least. Still, Mrs. Ford had a couple of warm-up jokes she'd painstakingly prepared, and she was bound to tell them. They fell flat. The audience sat so quietly one could hear a pin drop, and Mrs. Ford felt revulsion when she glanced at the rows of dull, unsmiling faces.

She turned to her program notes. "Well now," she said. "What have we here?"

"Ah! First on the program tonight, ladies and gentlemen, boys and girls, is Hannah-Maria Burns, who'll favor us with her jig-dancing!"

A roar went up from the crowd. Lulu, working at the coffee counter, blushed and ducked out of sight. The cheering threatened to swell into a standing ovation even before the performance, but it was soon quelled. Nothing happened and as the crowd quieted, the Canon's raspy whisper could be heard.

"... but I don't know why it's still on the program. She told us weeks ago she wouldn't do it! She's not on the program and never was; I don't know how it got on!"

Oscar Appleyard, who with Pat Parnell, was operating the curtains, sniggered into his hand.

"Oh dear," Mrs. Ford said. "It appears there's been a mistake on the program. But, the show must go on as they say in show business, and next for your delectation, ladies and gentlemen, boys and girls, 'Joe Caribou and his Caribou Rats'!"

A heavy groan rose from the audience which changed shortly to cheers and clapping when the Rats appeared with their "Medley of Yuletide songs". They were called back for several encores. Their sparse Christmas repertory was quickly exhausted, so they gave their admirers: "You are my Sunshine" and "Remember me".

Mrs. Prout, nervously pacing about in the wings was heard to exclaim of the last numbers done by the Rats, "Inappropriate, not at all in keeping wid Christmas."

"But dear," said Mr. Prout, "they're helping to make the concert a success."

"Oh, shut up, Patrice" she snapped. "'ow does me 'air look?"

Geoff, Nichol and Sergeant Sitter were next. They came

on dressed in blankets and Indian war paint, and were accorded a hearty round of applause. The Indians were almost mesmerized. Here were these white people who did nothing but drink and go about on mysterious and useless tasks day after day in Poontuk, suddenly transformed out of all their usual character. Just as the whites had wondered at the organization and function of the Tea Dance, so the natives wondered at the white man's goings-on now.

The Poontuk Trio as they called themselves, favored the audience with "Heap Big Smoke but No Fire". This was a deep throated comment on the trio's sexual prowess, but the applause kept the trio on stage for their encore of: "I want a Beer just like the Beer that Pickled Dear old Dad", where their harmony, more by good luck than good musicianship, since they'd never been able to achieve it in practice, brought them cheers from both the front of house and backstage.

Appleyard, manning the curtain, was more than appreciative: "Jeez, you guys, you soun' great...I'm not shittin' you, I really mean it.... you guys soun' great. Like a barbershop quartet or somethin'. Here, have a drink, I thin' I got enough lef'."

As Mr. Ford had predicted, the whole town was involved. A group of native boys did a takeoff on the Tea Dance, several Brothers from the hospital sang a medley of French Canadian songs, and got everybody to join in singing "Alouette".

Seated at the back of the hall were Frank, Fat Mary, and George.

"Jesus Christ!" said Frank. "I don't know why the hell I let you talk me into coming to dis place anyway. Let's go!"

"You're a vile, uneducated man, Frances, without a spark of appreciation for the arts," said George. He made a shift, and pulled a bottle from his back pocket. "Here, have a drink"

"Not now, gotta piss!"

One must remember that Frank and George always spoke as if each were totally deaf; and Frank's announcement came right in the middle of Mrs. Ford's announcement about the next act.

Frank was now in the aisle. He walked down toward the stage, paused, scratched his head, then came back to George and Fat Mary.

"Whar's the shit-house?" he demanded, at the top of his voice.

"I dunno, it's been changed from the last time we were here. You'll have to ask somebody."

"Well, gimme my hat."

"I ain't got your hat. Besides, what d'you need a hat for just to go to the shit-house?"

The program on stage stopped. The audience had turned to look at Frank and George, and as one man, extended arms and fingers to indicate Frank's goal, to which he shuffled without further adieu.

"Well, as I was saying," here Mrs. Ford glared at the departing figure of Frank and cleared her throat significantly. "As I was saying before the commotion, we have a special treat for you tonight." She smiled archly. "Yes, ladies and gentlemen! Brought in for tonight's performance at great expense to the management, and with no end of special arrangements, we are pleased to present Bing Crosby and the Andrews Sisters!"

If any applause were forthcoming from the audience, it was put down by a stentorian voice that announced for all to hear, "Jesus Christ, it's cold in the shit-house!"

"As I was saying," cried Mrs. Ford, upset. "As I was saying! We are pleased to announce the appearance of Bing Crosby and the Andrews Sisters. However, only two of the Andrews Sisters could make it for tonight's performance. Er, there wasn't enough room in the airplane. So here they are and lets give them a big, Fort Poontuk welcome."

A phonograph record hissed scratchily over the PA system and the tune "South America Take it Away" bellowed forth deafeningly, then quieted to nothing, as whispered cursing and exclamations filtered from backstage. At length the sound was restored and the announced trio bounced on stage.

The audience burst with spontaneous applause for the colorfully costumed persons, two huge women in sarongs and a man, but of course, it was the young weatherman, Nye-ee-sho, dancing about in a straw hat, Hawaiian shirt and carrying a pipe.

At the back of the hall, Frank's eyes bulged.

"My God, George," he exclaimed. "Do you see what I see up thar on the stage. Lookit' them women, partic'lar that one in blue. Jesus Christ! She must weigh at least a hunerd and fifty pounds." His face ballooned with lust.

"Take it easy, Francis," said George. He gave Fat Mary a wink and a squeeze. "You don't know those girls, who they are or where they come from."

"Who cares?" cried Frank. "That one woman thar might go a hunerd and fifty pounds."

The number on stage concluded, and Frank used the ensuing applause to make his way backstage.

It was Frank's good fortune to find the object of his excitement, the girl in blue, bent over and untying her high-heeled shoes.

He reached out and grabbed her by the fat of her buttock. It felt good!

He beamed like the summer sun. "Hey thar girl," he exalted. "How 'bout a little drink with ol' Frank?"

The girl immediately swung about. The yellow wig fell off and Frank stepped back in horror.

"Get away from me, you lecherous old bastard!" yelled Sitter, while the other woman - suddenly revealed as Parnell - and Geoff roared with laughter.

But Frank was already leaving the scene. In his confusion, he rushed onto the stage, as Mrs. Ford was announcing the next act. The audience clapped and shouted, and Frank was stunned to the spot at centre stage. Mrs. Ford turned and glared at him again.

"Frank!" she said sharply. "I've had enough of your tom-foolery. Just what are you doing here?"

Frank's eyes darted about maniacally, a cornered animal looking for a way out. "Er..I wuz.. that is... like" Then he seized an idea. "I wuz only lookin' for the shit-house!"

The audience was not prepared for what came next: The sombre darkened stage, and plangent recorded music for the much talked-about production of "The Bishop's Candlesticks".

The play opened quietly with several minutes of expository dialogue between Jean Trent, who played a serving girl, and Mrs. Prout, who played a shrewish housekeeper. Imperfect players both, they could scarcely be heard over the initial din of the crowd, still buzzing from Frank's antics. As the crowd quieted down, so did the players. The crowd could be seen leaning forward, perking its ears in an effort to find out what was going on. What was engaging these people on stage? But the effort was in vain. The audience became fidgety and murmurous.

"Jesus Christ, what the hell dey sayin'?" thundered a voice from the back of the hall. "Can't hear a God-damned ting!"

Order was restored with the appearance onstage of Canon Ford, playing the Bishop. Ford was in fine voice and his rich, assured delivery rallied the others. The play now caught the audience, most of whom had never in their lives seen its like. Soon the Bishop was left alone on stage, and a pin-drop could have been heard as he sat in his chair, sighed and fell asleep before a flickering fire.

At this point a reviewer might have observed that the

play "after a rather shaky start, settled down". It appeared at this juncture that a fine evening's entertainment would ensue. But fiasco unfortunately hung over the stage like a fallen angel, ready to wreak vengeance. For Constable Kenneth Button, playing the convict, from the onset was far too strong. He came on too loud, too bombastic. The mountain was climbed with his first speech and he had nowhere to go but down.

For thinking of the play and his part in it, Button had not slept a wink the night before. He'd dragged through the day, but felt calm enough, until somebody in all innocence had asked, "Well, Ken, you all ready for the play tonight?" It was the slam of a sledge-hammer into his stomach. He'd eaten some lunch, but couldn't manage dinner, couldn't eat, couldn't drink and had smoked an entire package of cigarettes. Changing into his costume for the part of the escaped convict, Button fervently hoped the stage would collapse, maybe somebody in the cast might have a heart attack, or the hotel would burn down, or there'd be a murder in the town, which he'd have to investigate immediately.

None of these things happened. A block of ice grew steadily where his stomach should have been. He felt himself prey to all kinds of vague aches, pains and fevers. Nausea accompanied his every move and threatened to bring him down.

"Concentrate, Concentrate!" he told himself, remembering the exhortations of Canon Ford.

And so he stood in the wings, racked with thrills of nervousness so strong he thought he would never move again. The Bishop alone on stage would say: "It was kind of her to think of that." That was his cue.

When he'd come to the hotel three hours ago, he thought he'd have time to apply make-up, dress, and then lie down. Because he felt a strange fatigue that, for all his nervousness, forced him to yawn almost constantly. How he wanted to lie down while there was still time, lie down and close his eyes for just a moment.

But the time flashed by like quick-silver. The program preceding the play was over in a heartbeat! He heard his play announced, and here he was in the wings. Jean Trent and Mrs. Prout were on.

Surely they had more to say than that! But they left the stage and the Bishop was alone. Button's nervousness was so strong he thought he might pass out. His heart was thumping. He couldn't seem to get enough air! He was suffocating!

"It was kind of her to think of that," said the Bishop. The script called for music at Button's entrance. In this particular production, the music could have been the melodramatic favorite, "The Slimy Viper". For what was this the audience saw? A tall, menacing figure in torn and dirty rags, head and eyes rolling, and teeth gnashing, advancing on the drowsy Bishop with a drawn knife.

Button was recognized. This was the man who, for most of the audience, meant troublesome authority. Here was the man who fined them for drinking, checked up on their fishing, hunting and trapping licenses, sent them off to jail in Fort Smith, suddenly seen sneaking across the stage and about to kill the Bishop! A howl of warning inextricably mixed with nervous laughter rocked the auditorium. The noise increased as the Convict drew nearer and nearer the Bishop.

Suddenly, the Convict lunged and seized the Bishop from behind.

"If you call out you are a dead man!" The words were screamed at the top of the voice, with such ferocity the tumult in the audience stopped.

The calm voice of the Bishop floated out over the enrapt audience. "Can I help you in any way?"

Then the Convict, again at the top of his voice, declared,

"give me food quickly, quickly, curse you!"

Now the audience was recovering from the Convict's initial outburst. Now they saw the Mountie menacing the Minister and demanding food at the point of a knife. Ho Ho! What was this? A few chuckles started from different parts of the audience, and continued as the play went on.

The Convict's big speech was approaching, and the audience was finding more and more to laugh about in the play.

The Convict the audience learned was a thief! In his own words, delivered at top volume, he said: "She was ill, we had no food. I could get no work. It was a bad year, and my wife, my Jeannette was ill, dying. So I stole! Yes! I stole to buy her food!"

Here the audience burst out laughing. The Mountie was telling everybody he stole.

The laughter grew louder, and - though it hardly seemed possible - so did Button's voice. An actor now, he would deliver his major speech though hell or the laughing audience should bar the way! It was a contest.

Appleyard agreed. Standing unsteadily in the wings, he saw the action as a baseball game. His buddy, the Mountie, stood against the antagonistic audience. Appleyard shouted encouragement to the man on stage.

"C'mon, Button! That's right. Give it to 'em! You can do 'er, Kenny-baby. 'Way to go!"

"God curse them all!" screamed the Convict, and he flung a joint of meat he'd been eating from the table.

Immediately there was a rush and grab by members of the audience to lay hands on this talisman from the stage.

The Bishop said, "My son, you have suffered much. But there is hope for all."

The Convict attempted a reply. In the din of the crowd and Appleyard's increasingly fervent exhortations from the wings, nothing could be heard. The Convict looked like a fish out of water, wide-eyed, his mouth opening and closing, but no sound coming out.

So then the crowd quieted; the Convict could now be heard; where the voice had been strong and passionate, it was now a thin, raspy squeak. "Hope, hope! Ha! Ha! Ha!" said the Convict.

In the wings, Jean Trent and Mrs. Prout sympathetically touched their throats. They had never heard such a horrendous case of laryngitis.

The remainder of the play was pure serendipity for most of the audience, who found Button's plight uproariously funny.

The curtain call proved a capper. The players came forward, joined hands and bowed. Not a sound from the audience. So the players, after exchanging expressions of alarm, bowed again, and this excited a few scattered titters. Then members of the audience, because they could think of nothing better to do, rose and started bowing back.

Chapter 20

Frozen Nose

"**I**f you people believe that the weather works in forty-year cycles, you're wrong," Trent remarked one day. "It's more like forty-one years." He smiled. "Anyway, the point I'm trying to make is that this winter is shaping up as one of the worst we've ever had, and that will make it just forty-one years after the winter of 1906, which is considered the worst of all in Canada. There wasn't any meteorological service in those days, but the word of mouth makes it a dandy. It rained all summer, particularly in the West. Then the first blizzard came early in November, and there was no let up until May. There were a couple of days when the Chinook blew, but this just melted the top of the snow, and then, when the cold weather came back in a day or two, ice four-inches thick, formed on the top of the snow. The cattle industry out West was practically knocked out, because with the wet summer, ranchers had difficulty getting the hay in. Now, I don't know what the weather maps looked like back in those days as there aren't any. But I'd bet money they'd look suspiciously like they do right now!"

December was not a particularly cold month in Fort Poontuk, but so far the temperature had gone down below 50 below (that was the week before the Christmas Concert, now known as "Ford's Fiasco") and it hadn't warmed up much since. Trent once again despaired of a visit from the warm wind this winter. The daily pilot balloon observations - the weathermen called them "pibals" - showed that, if there was any warm air around, it was sliding over the dome of the cold air on westerly winds, more than five miles straight up.

Trent was even suggesting a new record cold temperature might be set that winter, at Fort Poontuk. It was possible: The coldest weather of the Canadian winter was not usually in the high Arctic, but in the hinterland, just below the Arctic Circle. Trent thought, if he couldn't score marks analyzing warm winds, he might try for an investigation into the other extreme.

In any event, this meant more "pibals" had to be taken by Jerome Geoff. Because it was dark, a candle, enclosed in a Japanese lantern, was tied to the balloon. Then, for usually three-quarters of an hour, while the temperature hovered at forty below, Geoff followed the yellow star that marked the meandering of the balloon through the theodolite. Readings were taken each minute, marked by the sound of a timer-unit built into the theodolite shelter. Cold weather altered everything, and the warning sound of the buzzer now sounded like an extended breaking of wind. Persons passing by would hear it, followed by a muffled oath from Geoff and the brief flashlight's glow as he took the readings. Geoff had to keep the moisture of his breath from clouding the eye-piece, had to make sure his skin didn't touch, for it would stick painfully fast to the frigid metal. Between readings, he would stand back from the instrument, swatting his arms around his body in the classic exercise to maintain warmth until summoned again to take another reading by the drawn-out fart sound of the timing mechanism.

This time, he clapped his brow to the rubber eye-piece to watch the tiny yellow light, like an errant planet from another system, pause and then gradually merge and disappear into the star-sown firmament. Geoff was arrested by the sight. It was as if his balloon, now in shreds and fluttering earthward somewhere out there in the cold darkness had left his spirit up among the stars. Geoff grinned. The balloon had slipped the surly earth's atmosphere and had taken his soul to wander about into the sparkling filigree of the dark sky. The northern lights, a pale glow before, now rose from the northern horizon to play its emerald splendor across the universe. He watched and he listened. It was not possible that those efflorescent curtains of the aurora could sweep the way they did without sound. They were too grand, too stupendous to swish from the earth to the outermost red giant without sound. Frank and George had said they heard the aurora crackle. "Science be damned," they said. "We've heard 'em!" Geoff wondered as he strained his ears if the sound wasn't suggested by the mesmerizing spectacle. What difference did that make? For a man under hypnosis, the sound of the fire siren is just as real as his reaction to it. So Geoff had only to surrender up his will to the splendor of the night sky and eventually a message would come through.

"You going to stay out there all night?" asked Trent, wanting the readings of the balloon observation.

Trent switched on the yard light, and Geoff, walking toward the station was overwhelmed again. The previous night a light fall of snow had occurred. This time, it was genuine snow of the six-pointed-flake variety, not the grey, flinty ice crystals, which were the usual precipitation. These flakes, excited by the light, were glittering like diamonds, millions of them, at his feet. As he moved, they shot their tiny flashes, white and the most delicate pinks and blues, striking his eye from a thousand angles as his movement brought him into the varying sight lines of the flakes' infinite facets. He was dazzled and almost lost his way.

"Mr. Geoff, if you don't mind, this way," said Trent with elaborate impatience. "We don't want to be up all night."

'Am I the only one who notices these things?' Geoff asked himself. 'Am I the only one who is aware of what's going on around about us?' Had nobody else, Trent, his wife, Canon Ford, anybody, noticed the diamonds in the sky and on the ground? Are they all so inured to the splendor of things here in the north that they now take them for granted?

After working up the results of the "pibal" and giving them to Trent, Geoff stood quietly in the area between the station and his quarters. The yard-light was off, so the diamonds at his feet had disappeared and the shimmering aurora was beginning to pale. What light remained was streaking toward the centre of the sky, vanishing through an aperture into some unspeakably remote other universe. The sky blackened and the stars' glitter sharpened. The aurora had gone.

It grew colder, the night, darker. And to his utter amazement, Geoff found that the sky-soaring excitement he'd known a few moments ago had gone with the aurora and he was saddened; because it seemed that the brilliant celestial show he'd seen was but a meaningless chimera. The stars were watching him pitilessly, wanting to see how he'd react to the truth of the matter. The cold winter season is the reality, not the flaunting effulgence in the sky, and woe betide him who becomes confused. The aurora comes and goes, the snow sparkles, but the cold remains, and even the sun becomes a pallid, fleeting disc. One can only feel stupid for having ever thought that warmth and happiness were real things. Far to the East there was but the faintest touch of purplish light, not visible really, if one didn't look for it; less a light than a suggestion of what was supposed to happen. That was all of the sunrise that Fort Poontuk would enjoy today.

Then a cruel, invisible demon lunged out of the dark night and sank its fangs into the end of his nose, biting clean through. Geoff cried out and clamped his mitten to his face.

Lulu was waiting for him in his room. "Jesu' Chris'!" she said. "Yo gone and frozen your nose."

"What'll I do?" panicked Geoff. "My God, is the nose goin' to get gangrene and drop off?"

"No!" she fumed. "You so stupid about some tins. What were you doin' standin' out 'n da cold for so long? Yo' crazy or sometin'?"

"Just thinking about things," muttered Geoff. "What'll I

145

do? Rub it with snow! That's what you're supposed to do!"

"No," she said. "Yo' should put bear grease on it. Somethin' like dat. You've got to let it taw-out slowly. Dat's da main ting."

Half-facetiously he said, "I gotta better idea. Let me put it between your boobies."

"Okay," she said, as if she had been waiting for him to make the suggestion. Off came the heavy turtle-neck sweater to reveal her bosom, displayed in a black lace bra.

Geoff's eyes popped. "Where the hell you get that?"

"It's a French brassiere. Never had one like it. Yo' like it?"

"Never thought I'd see one in Poontuk! But who?"

"Clarence Crunk," said Lulu. "He gave it to me."

"What!" exclaimed Geoff. "The fat hulk gave you that? Guess he was trying to make amends, eh? I hear he almost tried to rape you once, in front of a bunch of priests or something."

She laughed. "No, it wasn't anytin' like dat. He likes me and he gives me tins. Like dis." With that, she cupped her breasts, admired them for a moment in their fancy integument, and then winked elaborately at him. "C'mon, let's fix dat frozen nose."

Chapter 21

Winter Patrol

That Wednesday, on the advice of Dr. Fleming, Clarence Crunk had come to the Single Men's quarters so that he could have some 'sits baths" prior to his being flown out on Friday for treatment of bleeding piles.

Crunk was fulfilled. At last, he was centre-stage in the major role of his life, the role he'd been born to play. Never had anyone more enjoyed poor health. He took up residence in the bathroom. Those wishing to relieve themselves simply had to put up with him as, up to his chin in hot water, he tirelessly declaimed on the infinite details of his latest affliction.

Even at dinner: "I tell you, it's terrible. I got up one morning and it was like somebody had rammed a hot poker up my ass. Oh the pain was almost too much to bear. My buttocks felt like two big boils about to burst with puss and blood. And they throbbed! It was embarrassing, I tell you. I had to come to town and go to Harry's place and order some Kotex. He asked me what size, and I said, I didn't know, I mean how am I to know it comes in different sizes? He says, "Well, who's it for?" and I tell him it ain't for nobody, it's for me - I mean what does he take me for? I don't buy Kotex - and he looks at me like I'm crazy.

"Oh, I blame the authorities in Edmonton for this. I told the old D. Met when he was here to get me some stuff, but I never heard nothing about it. And I ordered some special soft paper, not that sandpaper stuff that the government issues, but nothing came of it. It's terrible. Every time I go to the bathroom and wipe up afterward, it's like a cluster of grapes down there, all covered with blood..."

"Crunk! cried Salt. "For Christ's sake, will you shut up."

In his clumsy, bearish way, Crunk disrupted the entire routine. He only got out of the tub to eat and relieve himself, during the commission of which he raised such moans and groans that a visitor would have thought the bathroom were a torture chamber. Any questions raised prompted long and unflagging replies.

Crunk had to be persuaded indeed to leave the bathroom on the Friday evening when the plane arrived, so that the regular party could be held. Crunk spent the evening sulking in one corner of the room, a glowering, brooding presence, who, out of chagrin, refused to join with Joe Caribou and his Caribou Rats for the evening's dance music.

All were relieved when on its return trip Sunday, the plane carried off Clarence Crunk to Edmonton, and the Royal Alexandra Hospital.

In two weeks he returned, and made a special trip to town just to tell people about his operation, which he said, "was like giving birth to a wildcat...backwards."

Wintertime was also the most arduous time for Constable Kenneth Button. Locally, he was kept busiest during the summer months when all the trappers were in town. In the wintertime, except for the older people, the Army and other government people, the town was practically deserted. In the dead of winter, in early February, Button was required to make a patrol two hundred miles downstream of Fort Poontuk, to check on the health and welfare of the trappers camped along that route. The patrol had been set up long ago at a time of year when weather was usually at its coldest. The Constable's only companions were a Special Indian Police Constable, known as Old Mustard, and the sled dogs.

Button's patrol usually tried to reach a cabin to hole up for the night, but when this couldn't be done, they would build a lean-to, boil their tea, eat their bannock, toss fish to the dogs, and turn into their eider-down sleeping robes. In the cold and lonely sub-Arctic, Button would watch the aurora borealis sweep and shimmer across the sky, so full of life and movement in contrast to the dark, cold forest lying gloomily about him.

Button had leisure to think about some of the strange things that had happened last summer. There'd been a magician arrive in Fort Poontuk in an ancient flying boat. It was ridiculous. What had a professional magician been doing flying the Mackenzie route? There wasn't a nickel to be made in such an enterprise. Button had gone to the show. He had seen a rather amateurish performance: Flowers bursting out of the end of a cane; colored silks flying about at every turn; and, some card tricks. Had the show been mounted anywhere else, it would have been booed off the stage, but in entertainment-starved Fort Poontuk, the thing was a smash. Then there had been the magician's 'Lovely Assistant', a hard-looking blonde in the standard abbreviated costume and tatty, net stockings.

The whole town had turned out for the show. They had never seen anything like it. From the start; when the magician himself and his assistant posted themselves outside Harry Crum's hotel, and while she pounded on a big bass drum, he did his "Hurray! Hurray!" circus routine with a big bullhorn. To the end; when the assistant went into a labored tap dance that brought roars of approval from the crowd for several sweating encores.

Afterward, Button had talked with the magician, tried to get answers to some obvious questions that rose in his mind out of native curiosity as much as for his police report. How had the magician contracted to use Harry's hotel? Where had he come from, to where was he bound? And that ancient flying boat... was it really at one time used by a famed African explorer? All legitimate and certainly not suspicion-arousing questions, so far as Button was concerned. But the magician was evasive. Button got his answers, but no real information, and he tired of a kind of cat-and-mouse game that developed, more especially since he didn't know who was playing which role. His cop's instincts told him something was wrong.

Something was. By merest chance, Mr. Prout had checked his fur bins at the Hudson's Bay post after the show. The entire season's take of marten and mink furs was gone! Prout nearly had a heart attack. It was the redoubtable Mrs. Prout who had reported the theft to Button.

"I knew it!" shouted Button, who despite the woman's anguish, couldn't suppress a smile of triumph.

It all fell into place: The past winter had been one of the best in years for trapping, and Fort Poontuk was one of the major depots in the north for fur-gathering. A plum ripe for plucking. So, while the rubes were lured into the hotel, the weasel-faced little pilot, perhaps the brains of the whole operation, made off with the furs.

The theft had been carefully planned and executed. Even as Mrs. Prout spoke, Button could hear the engine of the flying boat sputtering into life. The thieves were taking off and taking the loot with them. There wasn't a moment to lose.

Button had pushed by the jabbering Mrs. Prout, roused Special Constable, Old Mustard, and in moments had been roaring out into the Mackenzie aboard the police scow.
Old Mustard had thought the boss had gone mad: Trying to catch an airplane with the scow?

They had charged out onto the broad bosom of the Mackenzie, the two 'kickers' raising a noise almost as loud as the aircraft's engine. A crowd began to gather along the riverbank. The watchers saw the scow close on the slowly taxiing flying boat, which, suddenly aware of its being pursued, raced off downstream, gathering speed that left the scow behind. But the plane didn't take off! The weather was flat calm, and without a puff of wind, the underpowered flying boat couldn't leave the river. The flying boat turned about and started on a collision course with the scow.

A cry of warning went up from those on the bank, and, as Old Mustard skillfully turned the scow from the flying boat's path, the cries of warning turned to cheers. But, collision wasn't intended. The pilot of the flying-boat was using the ruffled waters of the wake to loosen the river's grip on the hull. The flying boat was now churning upstream, splashing noisily through its own waves. The upper part of the hull cleared the surface, the wings seemed to reach out and flap. The wake became a straight-line, with sporadic Morse code written on the water. The flying-boat had looked for all the world at this moment like a mud-hen, frantically skipping across the water, flapping its wings, crying out, but failing to become airborne. The attempt was given up, and the hull sloshed back down to float depth.

Button and his man bore down again. The flying boat turned about and made another downstream run. Again, the hull lifted partly clear and the engine's roar shattered the calm air. Still the machine could not lift clear.

Back and forth the flying boat had raced, with the scow doggedly following, each machine snarling and whining, while those on the bank had "oh-ed" and "awh-ed" as if watching a hockey game with the action racing from one end of the rink to the other.

Now the action was broken off. The flying boat had made one final turn in the downstream direction and had started racing away, abandoning any further attempt to take off. But then the engine had spluttered, and stopped, then spluttered and stopped again. The flying boat was running out of gas! The mud-hen was now limping, and, gasping and wheezing, coming in.

The flying boat touched the shore. Instantly, the 'lovely assistant' still in costume, the magician and pilot had jumped out and had run up the bank. Then a fourth person, a young man, had suddenly appeared and had fled with the others. Gaining the top of the bank the escapers had stopped and stared. They were wild-eyed and tousled from their ordeal, and at a loss as to what to do next. The townspeople had simply stared back at them.

Button's scow had touched the bank. Button got out, and, shouting to Old Mustard to chase after the flying boat, which was now floating away downstream, had come charging up the bank.

The furtive foursome, with sudden resolution, had fled across the clear width of the Fort Poontuk settlement and had plunged into the bush.

"Hey, come back," had chorused Frank and George to their retreating figures. "What da hell you doin'?"

The better to make the escape, the assistant had shucked her high-heeled shoes.

"Let's just wait," said Button.

In minutes, cries of anguish could be heard from the cover of the bush: "EEEyow!"

"Help!"

"God! They're eatin' me alive!"

"You got us into this mess, now, what are you gonna do? Wise-guy!"

"Shut up, willya! We gotta get outa this!"

One by one, they had emerged, each with a nimbus of bloodthirsty insects about his head, at which each batted and impotently waved. Walking clear of the bush, they had raised their hands in total surrender.

"Don't shoot" the magician had said. "We'll come quietly."

Button had said: "I don't believe it."

He had put them all in detention quarters but didn't bother to lock them up. As a matter of course, he had let them rove around town completely unguarded. They had been as secure in Fort Poontuk as in the most formidable

2233322232233233332223

prison in Canada.

The 'lovely' assistant had come to Button as soon as she conveniently could.

"All alone up here in the north," she said. "You must get awfully lonesome for a white girl." She had seated herself in his office following their interrogation session. She had reached out and had run her hand over her thigh. "These net stockings are such a mess. Perhaps I'd better take them off."

Which she had proceeded to do. She had then smiled when she looked at his face and spoken again softly: "Maybe, ah...some arrangement could be worked out. I mean, I'm sure it must get awfully lonesome for you sleeping here all by yourself with nobody to talk to or.. you know...keep your back warm. Know what I mean?"

She had got up and had perched herself on the edge of his chair.

"Lookit," she had continued, while moving her fingers over her naked thighs. "Those damn flies sure make a mess of a girl's legs, don't they?"

He didn't say anything.

"In fact," she had continued. "I'm bitten all over! Wanna see?"

'She's almost old enough to be my mother', Button had thought.

Finally, he spoke. "No," he had responded. "That's okay."

Suddenly, he had scooped her up into his arms and started carrying her off into his bedroom. She had giggled, and thrashed her legs in mock resistance. "Oooh," she had enthused. "What's a Mountie doing, taking a girl to his bedroom?"

Afterward, Button had said simply: "No deals, no arrangements."

She had smiled contentedly. "That's okay. No hard

153

feelings."

Two days later, the RCMP plane had arrived from Fort Smith to take the thieves into more conventional custody.

Button roused in his sleeping bag. His dream of the summer's strange escapade had turned wet. He stole a look outside. The searingly cold air struck him in the face like a slap. He couldn't believe it for a moment. To be dashed from the voluptuous dream of the blonde to the harsh reality of the present situation left his senses muddled. For a giddy moment, he didn't know where he was; one part of him strained to return to the summertime episode, another clamored for realism to face the situation. Button retreated into the odoriferous warmth of his sleeping bag, and shut out the cold, whose icy fingers now tore at his face. He tried to return to the dream, but the clamorous voice would not have it. In his brief look out of his sleeping bag, Button had seen the grey streaks of dawn's early light dimming the stars. In a little while, it would be time to go through the dreadful routine of cooking the morning meal, eating, packing, harnessing the dogs, and proceeding one more day into the pitiless north.

The totally dark period lasted but a short time in Fort Poontuk, and when Button returned in late February, the sun was shining and bright.

Button and his Special Constable looked a mess. Their faces were wind-burned to a deep brown that had erased racial differences, their lips were chapped and swollen, their eyes, bloodshot, their noses and cheeks splotched and cracked from frostbite.

They could not help but smile - and in so doing, open bleeding cracks in their lips - as they were welcomed back. Because they had news, in the form of letters or oral reports from the men on the trap-lines to their wives or girl-friends, news about how the trapping was going, when they'd be coming in, how they felt, how the weather was, things that had happened to them, or things that should have happened but didn't, no treasure ship of old ever hove into harbor to a heartier reception.

As a fitting climax to the patrol, the dog-team was driven to the upstream end of the town and then raced down. In their excitement the dogs yipped and barked, each coughing a penny-puff of moisture into the crystalline air. From round about, people emerged from their cabins, shucking themselves into their parkas and exclaiming as the team raced by. The whole procession headed for the auditorium of Harry Crum's hotel.

The heat of the place almost overwhelmed Button as he walked in. It was not overly warm in the auditorium, but Button, having been subjected to temperatures never warmer than ten below for almost a month, wasted no time in getting out of his navy-blue parka and heavy woolen turtle-necked sweater. Similarly, those coming in removed their heavy outer garments and the auditorium took on the appearance of a fall rummage sale.

Both Old Mustard (not really that old, but afflicted with a trick back that caused him to crouch forward) and Button were lean and hard as wildcats. During their month together, jogging all day long, sleeping out under the most rigorous conditions, they had lived deprived of all creature comforts. Their condition put them in good stead.

Before they were able to relax, they had to spend the rest of the day dispensing the news and gossip from the trap line. The trapping was going good, or going bad as the case might be. Antoine wanted his wife to know he'd not been lucky with the marten, but he was catching lots of flying squirrels, which news, because the fur of these animals was regarded as trash, brought guffaws of derision from the crowd, and mortification to poor Antoine's wife. Frozway LaViolette had cut off the end of his thumb in a trap, but the wound was healing okay. There was news of the predations of wolverines, movement of caribou, snowfall, sickness and health.

Lulu along with some of the other women had prepared tea and coffee and laid out some sweet cookies that she'd inveigled from Scotty.

Button, sitting on a table and idly swinging a leg, was chatting quietly. Despite his growing fatigue, he was in no hurry to leave. Lulu had brought him coffee and some cookies, and he watched her as she moved about in the kitchen. Now and then their eyes met, though most often Button was appreciating the bulges in her sweater and ski-pants, and watched these phenomena as if mesmerized: He was too tired to play it cagily.

Chapter 22

Blizzard

It had struck Jerome Geoff so unexpectedly, so shockingly, that even now, a day after the occurrence, his mind was still in turmoil. A turmoil without resolution that had knocked down and dragged out cool reason and left only surprising and unaccustomed thoughts about murder, beatings and maimings. His brains were on fire, his guts were in knots and his veins flowed with venom and bile.

The condition had been brought about by accident. He wished to God it had never happened at all. He'd come from his room. Parnell and Nichol were talking in the kitchen over coffee. Their voices, held low, nevertheless could not conceal the tone of eager conspiracy, and Lulu's name kept cropping up. Geoff crept closer to the kitchen door. A part of him said he was better off leaving the situation alone - a weird presentiment as it turned out - better to forget it and walk away. Part of him said that, but another part, the part that lead to his escapades in Edmonton, the part that had urged him onto the frozen river just before break-up, that part won over. If he'd gone into the kitchen, he was sure the conversation would have stopped. This, he didn't want to happen. So, like a thief, he flattened against the wall and craned to hear.

Parnell's voice: "As you know, I hold Hannah-Maria, er, Lulu, very dear to my heart." He and Nichol chuckled quietly and intimately between them.

Nichol started to say something but was interrupted by

Parnell. Parnell had the floor and was not about to yield.

"I've 'known' the colleen myself of course," Parnell continued. "And I felt I 'knew' her - in the other sense of course, fairly well. But I do not understand the way she's carrying on now. It's not in character, but who understands women."

"That's right, Pat" said Nichol as conciliatory as ever. "They're hard to figure. Still, Lulu is quite a dish... like I had an experience once.."

"One thing about her," interrupted Parnell again. "She is sort of moral in her way. If she was going with one guy she never fooled around with any others. Until now, when she goes and shacks up with the Mountie. Oooooeeee!"

Geoff couldn't stand it. His ears had stretched like two antennae to gobble up every word, and each word had fanned the fires of rage to irresistible ferocity.

He charged into the kitchen, seized Parnell by the collar and shouted," You filthy bastard! Why don't you shut your filthy God-damn mouth!"

He even cocked his fist, but Nichol seized his arm. "Hey, Jerry," said Nichol urgently. "What's the matter? Take it easy, for God's sake."

"Yeah, if you wanna fight, why don't we step outside right now," said Parnell, recovering from the attack. For lack of something better to do he kept brushing at his tunic sleeves. "What's got into you anyway?"

That was the question. What had got into him? The great intellectual from the University of Alberta, the painter, wit, student of meteorology, philosophy and anthropology was suddenly cast into the role of beer-room brawler to defend the name of a slut. That's what he'd fallen to. The man who'd seen the Green Flash - and how many millions upon millions go through life without ever a glimpse of that wondrous thing - the man who'd marveled at the beauties of heaven and earth, whose mind was enrapt in the wonder and mystery of life, earth and sky, Ganymede! Revealed to have feet of mouldering clay.

Because he felt it was expected of him, Geoff suddenly loosed a dry, mirthless cackle. Nichol, and Parnell, who'd been watching him suspiciously, now exchanged glances and went out.

It was the first bout of jealousy that Geoff had ever known. It was a madness, excited by some dark side of his own soul. As the tongue is jammed into the cavity in sure knowledge that pain will result, so Geoff permitted his mind to dwell on Lulu - his Lulu! - moaning under Button's lean and heaving body, or mounting him and gyrating in shameless abandon, screaming her head off. Is that how those two signalmen found out about it? Had they gone by Button's place the other night and heard the sounds of their lovemaking? Was that how they'd found out?

Geoff jammed his face down into his pillow, pulled the sheets over his head as if to shut out the world, and consumed himself in hellish green flames. But there was one little imp that kept stabbing at his psyche, chuckling and gloating with each wound; an imp that would not be put down by rationalizations, dreams of purifying flames or sweet forgetfulness. It said: "You're not man enough, so she's gone to another!" As he'd heard Parnell say, "Geoff has been out-cocked!"

Sleep would not come even though he was so exhausted he couldn't summon the strength to turn off the radio. It was playing: "Your Cheatin' Heart."

The next evening, Lulu came to see him. He was aghast at the brazenness of the creature. He stared at her in utter amazement as she walked in, smiling and assured, as if nothing had happened, as if unaware of the violent emotion that distorted his features and must, he was sure, be permeating the atmosphere around him.

Before she had taken off her parka, he asked: "Where have you been the past couple of days?"

She smile narrowed a little. "Why do you want to know?"

"Well, I rather thought we had an understanding, you and I about certain things and I..."

"I've been to Ken Button's"

Geoff couldn't believe his ears. "You admit it!" he cried. "You admit you went over there to FUCK the Mountie!" He'd never used that word before, not even in all-male company. He'd been taught by his Uncle Bert that it was a bad word with a bad sound, and its unrestricted use could stunt one's vocabulary. But in his passion, Geoff wanted it. The word fuck suited his mood because it employed the entire mouth, the labiodental then the guttural, bridged by the resonant vowel marching across the roof of the mouth. "That's all you bloody well ever think about, isn't it? Fucking!"

"What's da madder?" she asked, pursing her lips to restrain a laugh.

"What's the matter? What's the matter! Listen to this

dame!" said Geoff, starting to pace. "You've got to be nuts. What am I a stone or something? I thought we were like 'going together' and had some consideration for each other's feelings. Like the time you got mad and hit me when I got drunk. Remember that time? Well now what the hell am I to do? What am I to feel when you go off to the Mounted Police barracks to fuck!" He threw up his hands. "What's the matter? she says!"

"Will yo' listen to me?"

"No!" exploded Geoff. "You listen to me. What are you anyway? Some kind of trollop, some kind of whore, eh? Because that's how I feel about it. That's right. The minute my back is turned you go sneaking off. You're like those bloody Eskimo women who sleep with any visiting man. But at least that's the custom of the people. It's a sign of courtesy. What's your excuse?"

Lulu hid a smile behind her hand.

Geoff fumed, "This isn't funny, Lulu. You should be ashamed!"

"Would yo' listen to me?"

"Alright" he said sulkily. "Speak your bloody piece."

"I jus' felt sorry for Ken Button, dat's all" began Lulu. "He likes me... of course, all da men do... I can't help dat... but he never done nuttin'. He'd been out all da time on da patrol when it was so cold, so lonely and everytin' and he comes back to nobody. Even Old Mustard has a wife to fix him dinner and sleep wid him. But Ken Button got nuttin'. I felt pretty bad for him at Harry Crum's. So I went over and fixed some coffee and hotcakes with lots of bacon and maple syrup. I tink he really liked it."

Geoff laughed bitterly. "Ha! I'll bet he liked the second course even better, eh?"

"What's the madder wid' you?" sighed Lulu. "Is that all you can tink about?"

"All I ever think about! Listen to her! Listen you: It was you...not me...that went sneaking out for a little bit of..."

"But dat wasn't da only reason," said Lulu. "Don't you see. I tol' you already. He was tired out n' alone over dere."

"So what, for God's sake!" said Geoff. "You know what you did. You felt sorry for him, so you let him fuck you. God!"

"Alright, yes, I did" said Lulu, looking askance at Geoff. There was a persistent smile flirting with her lips, and the dim light cast her face in intriguing shadows. Geoff felt the strength and steel of his moral indignation crumbling before a siege of concupiscence. He felt that unless he sustained his rage, somehow or other, he'd sink into a tearful, unmanly state.

"Well, let me tell you something," he barked. "You know what they call women like you back where I come from?"

"I don' care," interjected Lulu. "Because we're not back where you come from, Heironymous Geoff. We are here, in Fort Poontuk. Dere's a difference."

"But..I.."

"Why don' yo' jus forget it," she said, turning her huge black eyes on him, arrogant in the panache of her beauty. "Yo' makin' too much of da whole ting'. I'm here tonight. Here wid you."

Geoff sat down, purged and shriven. He stared at the

floor. "It doesn't seem right," he muttered, barely audibly. Lulu stood up and took off her parka.

"Hey", she exclaimed brightly," I got on dat brassiere dat Clarence Crunk gave me. Jus for you."

She grinned and turned out the light. In bed, under the covers, she beckoned to him, and he flung himself into her arms. Ardently and eagerly, he kissed and caressed her, savoring the odor of tanned leather and woodsmoke.

"Take it easy," moaned Lulu. "I'm sore all over."

Winter was far from over in Fort Poontuk. A fierce blizzard smote the settlement. Scotty, going to fetch a gallon-can of diesel fuel, almost lost his way, though it wasn't more than fifty feet from the door to the oil tank. For the air was choked with knife-edged crystalline flakes that rose up from the ground, fell from the sky and, driven by the howling wind, swirled about the wayfarer, monstrously blocking up eyes and nose and taking one's breath. The blizzard lasted two days, during which, the town was taken away from its inhabitants. To look outside was to see nothing but undefined whiteness during the brief daylight period, and blackness at night with an eerie and persistent 'tap-tap', like frozen fingertips on the windowpane, etched upon the wind's unmitigated howling. Social intercourse ceased completely. Nobody ventured out unless it was necessary, for without references, one could stagger about in the cold white fog for too long, and it would not have been the first time that some one had died of exposure within a few yards of his own home.

Paul Salt took a drink, and another. When the mellowness arrived, he felt justified. What else was one to do with the blizzard howling outside? And the blizzard had even put a stop to the interminable poker game in the common room. Another drink.

He was thinking about Jean Trent. He was always thinking about her, about her brownish eyes with the golden flecks, about the suggestion of down on her upper lip, her quick smile and dimples, her body.

Her body! Salt felt a twinge of self-loathing, as though he had entertained carnal thoughts about his mother. After all the time that Jean had spent with him, trying to straighten him out. After all her sweet and kind attention, and above all her bravery. For what would happen, or could happen yet if Trent were to walk in on them. After all this, all he could think about was getting into her pants.

"A hard-on ain't got no conscience," he muttered, and then chuckled at his wit and wisdom.

Salt took another drink. And another, and thought about the strange relationship he'd managed throughout the winter. He thought about it all through the second day of the blizzard.

In the evening, the wind died down, and Salt staggered to the window to confirm what his drink-dulled hearing had slowly communicated: That the blizzard was over.

Salt was delighted with what he saw. The wind-rippled snow, inexpressibly white, scintillated in the starlight. He stepped back, danced a few steps, and almost fell. But he laughed it off. Because during the day, he had managed to convince himself, and the whiskey had not deterred him from this conclusion, that it was a certainty that Jean was thinking of him the same way he was thinking of her. What the hell! Maybe she was as hard up as he was. Maybe Trent was a dud in the sack, so bad that that was why he spent all his time in his office with his arithmetic and weather maps.

Salt gave himself a glancing blow on the side of the head. Why didn't he see the situation so clearly before? Of course, that's why Jean had been so good about his visits. She was climbing the walls, but was too much a lady to come right out and say anything! It was up to Salt to make the first move.

"Boy, I bet she thinks I'm really stupid." Salt said to himself.

With sudden determination, he put on his parka, his mukluks and gloves, and checked his flashlight. Outside, the air struck him like a dash of cold water in his face, and he pulled the drawstrings of his hood tighter. He looked around: Trent was working, as usual, at the station. He turned and headed for Jean's place.

After the extreme cold of the outside, the Trent living room was hot and he could feel the liquor he'd drunk even more.

He wanted to tell her something, but he wasn't sure what he was saying. When he'd come in she'd given him a funny look, wrapped in a smile, but it was not the look he'd expected of a passionate female with hot pants for him. He was taken aback.

As he spoke, he heard the words coming to him as from a different source, to the obvious amusement of Jean, whose face kept going out of focus and jumping like a film that has skipped the sprocket.

He gave it up. He stopped, and still in his parka he stood still behind the sofa and drew circles in the nap with his fingertip. His ears seemed on fire, they buzzed.

Then she walked toward him, spread her arms and gave his shoulders a strong hug. She was almost as tall as he. Her head rested for a moment on his shoulder and he could feel the fine silkiness of her hair. He raised a hand to touch it gingerly, so soft it was, and so filled with fragrance. The flesh of her arms was smooth, cool and yielding, and his hands roved over her shoulders and down her back. He pressed her bosom to him.

"Kiss me, kiss me like you do," he pleaded.

He moved his head about, his lips seeking hers. "Jean, Jean" he called softly but urgently.

Again, her voice fell on his ear strangely. It was so quiet. "Paul, I think we'd better calm down a little, huh?"

He moved his mouth down the side of her neck, to the softness there and he ravened it with kisses. His hands went down her back and over her buttocks, as he pushed her against the sofa.

"Paul!"

He was pushed into a chair. Jean stood over him but he couldn't read her expression. The film had slipped the sprockets again.

She was speaking quietly to him, but in his intoxication and befuddlement, not everything she said was registered: "It's my fault, Paul...I should have acted my age and leveled with you...something like this was bound to happen...I'm not a tease, Paul...we haven't enough room to play around....this town!" She flung out her hand in a histrionic gesture. Her voice dropped as she moved away from him. "You had better go now," she concluded.

He stumbled to his feet, clumsy in his oversized parka, and braced himself on the arm of the chair. He opened his mouth to speak but only a throaty single syllable blurted out. The room reeled as he turned and staggered to the front door.

He rushed out, tripped on the steps, and fell to the ground. He heard the door close behind him. He got to his feet and with a belligerent detachment, watched as the white ground rushed up to smack him in the face. Up again; and everything started going around his head as if he were on a sickening crazy house merry-go-round of shimmering green from the Northern Lights, the twinkling stars on the black velvet sky, and the bone-white snow.

He was on the road. "Jesus, it's cold!" he shouted. As he continued to stagger almost to the river's edge on his left and then an equal distance to his right. He was much drunker than he realized.

There was something black and ugly welling up inside him, something he wanted concealed and forgotten. But the cold pierced through the drunkenness and ripped aside the curtain.

"Oh God!" he cried. "I tried to rape her!"

He had kissed her face and neck. She had struggled to get away from him, because he was little and ugly and unshaven and a drunken bastard who tried to feel her up and grab her between the legs.

His hands flew to his face. His parka hood was knocked back as he thumped his head on either side as if to drive out the vision. He fell to the ground, heavily this time, and felt a stab of pain in his elbow.

"It's all right. It's all right," a voice said. He listened intently and made a half-hearted effort from his prone position to look around. He couldn't see anybody and abandoned the scan. Don't worry about it now, he thought, just relax. He made no further effort to get up, and let the heaviness of his limbs persuade the rest of him to lie still.

He felt himself falling over backwards into a black, warm abyss. He'd had this happen before. Once, when he'd been drinking for two days it had happened. He'd felt himself falling backward into this same black hole. It had frightened him then. He'd resisted, because it wasn't just passing out from too much booze, it was something evil and dangerous. Now, he didn't care. He felt himself falling deeper into the blackness.

"I don't give a shit!" he muttered. "Let's ride 'er out and see what happens." Thus committed, he felt snug, secure, and very, very sleepy.

Taking the weather observation at midnight, Trent whistled with surprise. The thermometer showed fifty degrees below zero.

Trent was always hard to wake up, so his wife shook and shouted at him unmercifully: "Cy! Cy! Will you wake up! It's happening!"

"What...what? Go away and leave me alone."

But outside stimulus were beginning to penetrate his comatose defenses and his eyes popped. He became suddenly aware of a great roaring and unrest all around. The walls of the house trembled, the windows rattled, and sinuous drafts were slithering about.

"Not another bloody blizzard," said Trent. "I didn't call it."

"No, Cy, it's not a blizzard. It's your wind...the warm, katabatic wind, the Chinook, go and see for yourself. It's wonderful!"

Trent's features brightened as he struggled into his clothes and rushed through the front door.

The wind, as if it had been leaning on the door, came bursting in, warm and exuberant, scattering papers willy-nilly and pouring in with such a rush as to blow the house to pieces.

Outside, the wind, for all its strength, fell like a caress on the cheek. The sky looked softer and seemed bigger, filled as it was with thick, unmoving clouds, very high and stretched like white buttresses across the firmament.

"The katabatic wind at last!" yelled Trent, and he rushed down the footpath to the road. The snow was beginning to soften. "Jean, I've got to get to the station," he shouted as he hurried off down the road.

Trent almost tripped over the parka-clad figure of Paul Salt lying in the road. Trent bent over the supine figure and looked into Salt's face.

"Salt! What's the matter with you? Get up!"

No answer.

Trent put his hands in Salt's armpits and hauled him to his feet.

"Drunk again, eh?"

Salt's head swiveled on his neck. Then his entire body stiffened in Trent's arms. "What? Where am I?"

"You're sleeping in the middle of the road, you dumb bunny, and you almost got run over by me."

"You mean like...I'm not dead?"

Trent threw back his head and guffawed. "No, you're not dead. But you're in Paradise, just the same. Take off the parka, Salt! It's springtime in Fort Poontuk. The katabatic wind, the Chinook, has arrived." Trent pointed excitedly and said," Look, water's running off your place." He left Salt and went sprinting up the road. On top of the radio station the anemometer cups were whirling so fast they became a flashing blur.

Salt let the wind push him this way and that. It amused him. It was soft and warm, and he felt good. He had no hangover, and his head, long experience had taught, should have been a thumping agony to match his low mood. But he felt good.

The riverbed, because of the wind-whipped snow, resembled a vast witches' cauldron from which thin wisps dashed across the road.

In her doorway, Jean Trent stood, her arms folded against the wind. Salt waved to her, and she waved back.
He turned and walked home, his head full of rioting thoughts, questions and intimations; and he was unaware that his eyes were flooded.

Chapter 23

Back to the Outside

Time was running out for the two weathermen's sojourn in Fort Poontuk. Edmonton informed them that they would be leaving on the first airplane in May. Geoff was to be replaced by another weather observer and Trent's program would be discontinued.

Trent's paper on the katabatic wind, Chinook phenomenon at Poontuk excited little interest, although it was grudgingly admitted that a rise in temperature from 50 below zero to 35 degrees Fahrenheit above in a matter of a few hours was spectacular. But the reason for it's happening at all on the occasion recorded by Trent was wrapped in mystery. The weather map on that occasion was similar to many maps when the wind did not occur. In fact, there had been previous instances where conditions seemed far more favorable for the wind's development, but then nothing had happened. So, the mystery remained; Dame Nature had taunted and flaunted, but revealed nothing.

During the three days the wind held, Trent had the time of his life, plotting the maps, taking the reading from his robot stations, and boring anyone who would listen to him. He took Salt by the arm and led him to the maps to show him the isobars, fronts and upper-air conditions that had nurtured the wind. The wind was a tremendous phenomenon when one considered the unspeakably vast energy required to raise the temperature that much in that brief span of time. When Trent's explanation was done, Salt, who'd listened to the harangue with a bemused expression, extended his hand and said he wanted to apologize to Trent for what had happened in the past. He didn't want Trent to go away with bad blood between them.

Trent was puzzled, and more especially a few days later when, in conversation with Canon Ford, he found out that Salt had approached the cleric wanting to know about miracles and salvation. Canon Ford noted that Paul Salt felicitously bore the name of a Christian saint, who'd had an abrupt change in character on the road to Damascus. "And where do you think Paul Salt's road to Damascus may have been, Trent?" he asked. Trent hadn't the foggiest idea.

Jerome Geoff was beginning to think that perhaps last summer's run in with Uncle Felix and Lulu's removal from the Fort Poontuk scene had not only spared his eyesight, but perhaps his life. For his love life with Lulu, she the hyper-mammiferous, narrow-waisted, flare-hipped, long-legged apotheosis of desire, was turning his sexual fantasies into a nightmare. At various times, Geoff thought she was trying to get pregnant by him, and get herself a trip to the Outside by forcing him into the decent course of action. Then he considered it was more likely she'd gone nymphomaniac; maybe she had some Eskimo blood and got turned on, in response to some deep biological urge, by the strengthening sun and the longer days. She was Eurydice, escaped from the underworld and insatiable, with her appetite growing by what it fed on. Geoff couldn't keep up, despite all efforts to maintain his virility; for no matter how many scrambled eggs he had in the morning, how many vitamin pills, cans of smoked oysters, thoughts and dreams and stimulus from the men's magazines that littered the common room, he was, slowly but irrevocably, going down hill.

"Why do you want to look at dem magazines?" Lulu asked disgustedly. "Look, I got bigger boobies dan dey have." She proceeded to demonstrate; unhooking her prized French bra, then cupping and kneading her breasts, while she smiled at him and licked her lips.

She moved her naked body on top of his, spread her legs and slipped her hands under his buttocks. She whispered in his ear, and when no response came - Geoff was worn out - she changed her position. After a time, he did respond to fevered kisses on his neck and shoulders and an insistent tongue in his navel.

"Geoff", said Trent one day. "You're not looking at all well. You got the 'flu or something?"

"No, I'm alright. Just a little tired, that's all."

One evening, after stepping into the shoulder-high shelter that surrounded the theodolite, arms wrapped around his knees, almost toppling him.

"I been waitin' for you," said Lulu. "C'mon, let's do it here."

She was almost breathless with excitement and couldn't be put off. So, while Geoff made a pretense of following the weather-balloon, dutifully putting his eye to the theodolite whenever the buzzer gave its obscene sound, and waving to the occasional passers-by on the road, Lulu, her ski pants down at her ankles, ground her buttocks into Geoff's loins.

Later, when he returned to his room, she was there.

Immediately he came in, she flung off the bedclothes and by various postures, indicated her desires. After that, Lulu roused him for a session over the back of a chair, and still later, when she thought all was quiet in the quarters, she coaxed him into the bathtub. She finally left, leaving him blissfully floating in the tub, where Salt found him in the morning, to tell him he had a visitor in his room. It was Lulu, who said, as he came gingerly into the room (it was the punch line from a joke about Cleopatra he'd told her) "Hi dere. I'm not prone to argue!"

"Oh now," said Trent. "I'm really getting worried about you, Jerry. What's the trouble?"

"No, it's okay," said Geoff. "It's just that I'm not getting enough sleep. And my eyes are starting to bother me again."

"Well, there's no use killing yourself. Look, take the day off. I'll work the afternoon, get these weather abstracts done and do the "pibal". And if you don't start feeling better soon, you'd better go see Doc Fleming."

Geoff thought he'd sleep for a week. His repose lasted about two hours, because, when Lulu found Trent doing the "pibal", she rushed to Geoff's room and leaped into bed with him. "Now we got all afternoon and the night to 'do it'", she said, sparkling with salacious anticipation.

In his continuing effort to conserve strength and energy, Geoff found it best advised to work rather than take the afternoons off.

Geoff thought he would never see the day when he'd be brought to his present state. His dreams of Lulu had seen her at one time as a sprightly succubus, but now she was resolved as a huge, gaping rictus of destruction that would gobble him up body and soul.

"Lulu, listen to me," said Geoff late one night. "I've got to get some rest. I don't know how you can keep it up. I'm worn out, I tell you! Look at me. I've lost weight, got bags under my eyes, can't sleep....I'm a mess."

"Don't you like me anymore," she asked.

"Liking you or not liking you is not the question, Lulu. It's this never-ending sexual intercourse, morning, noon and night. I can't take it anymore, I tell you. Why can't we just get together and talk now and then?"

"What would you like to talk about?"

"Oh, I dunno, anything" he said. "For example, if you were pregnant, would you want me to marry you?"

She laughed loudly. "No! I wouldn't want you to marry me, why should I? Day're my kids. Anyway, if I was ugly, you men would have nutin' to do wid me. But I've got dis body. You and da udders couldn't keep your hands off. I don't tink any man can. So, if I got married, it would only make trouble when udder guys came around." She smiled and shrugged her shoulders. "Oh, I dunno. Maybe when I'm fifty years-old or sometin'." She looked at Geoff intently. "You know, you guys are like the wind you were talkin' bout; but you're only here for a little while, den you go. But Hannah-Maria stays." She moved her body closer to his and whispered in his ear, "And dat's enough talk!"

When it was over and he was about to slip away into a deep sleep, she leaned over him and asked, "Now, are you sorry for dose tings you said 'bout me and Kennet' Button?"

That was the last that Geoff ever saw of Lulu. She got

up and walked out and didn't come back. After a couple of days, Geoff wryly admitted to himself that he had a good chance at last to rest up, he thought of going to the old crone's cabin for a final fling, but this didn't seem meet.

The peculiar northern sun was exerting its special influence, warming the arid atmosphere not so much through strength than through persistence, which had banished the snow from the community leaving only that which cowered in the dark forest. The ice on the Mackenzie river, ravaged as it had been by the unusual Chinook, was more pitted, sleazier and grayer than anyone could remember at this time of the year. An early break-up was anticipated: Already there were deep, sepulchral groans being heaved up from the riverbed.

Geoff's replacement, Milo Smithers, arrived, and found the sublimating Geoff to be one of the most attentive, good natured and peerless persons he'd ever met in the Canadian Civil Service. Smithers wore horn-rimmed glasses, was buck-toothed, a snoop, and possessed of an inexhaustible and discursive curiosity.

Smithers learned the dangers of generating hydrogen gas, the peculiarities of Fort Poontuk weather instrumentation and the intricacies of the theodolite. Then, he ventured further afield, wandering the town and the river bed.

Each day he came in with new questions or observations:

"Hey, who are those two old guys that sing the religious songs all the time?"

"I've seen some hen-pecked guys in my time, but that poor guy at the Hudson's Bay store...man!"

"What exactly does Harry Crum do in this town?"

176

"When does the river break up?...when does it freeze up?...what's the coldest it ever got here?...the warmest? How often does that Chinook wind blow here?"

One evening he came in and sat down, a stunned expression on his face. Lulu, it appeared, was back in circulation.

Geoff and the Trents arrived at the Poontuk airport, as did most who departed, hung over from the previous night's going-away party. Bonnycastle and Sitter were there with the jeep to see them off, but nobody knew quite what to say. Outside, because of their different backgrounds and occupations, they'd probably never have seen each other. The camaraderie of Fort Poontuk society was something that could not be exported. So everybody felt relieved when those who were leaving were aboard the airplane, and those who were staying were journeying back to the town.

The plane bounced to the end of the runway. After the esoteric preliminaries to flight - the engines roaring up and sputtering down, fire belching from the exhausts - the plane sped forward.

On a stout northerly wind, the plane climbed quickly and the vast panorama of the north exploded outward until it fused in the far distance with the sky. The plane banked to the right and headed on a southerly course that took it over Fort Poontuk. No people could be seen, only the uncertain scattering of buildings in the tiny riverside niche. Then the niche was swallowed up by the forest, so totally and quickly as to leave one wondering if Fort Poontuk had ever been there at all.

THE END

William Richard Matheson

ABOUT THE AUTHOR
William Richard (Bill) Matheson - 1926 – 2006

Beloved Alberta television weatherman, radio talk show host, news broadcaster and award-winning playwright, Bill Matheson wrote the manuscript for A Year Down North in 1976 when he worked briefly as weekend weatherman at New York City's WABC.

This fictional account draws on Bill's work as a meteorological assistant for the Department of Transportation at Fort Simpson, NT following his release from the Canadian Army after WWII in the 1940's.

In Lethbridge, Alberta from the early 1950's until 1974, Bill was the television weatherman at CJLH, a news broadcaster, and host of a radio talk show, known as "The Phone Bill Show" at CJOC Radio station, co-hosted by Terry Bland.

In 1976, Bill left New York and returned to Alberta, to Edmonton, to be the television weatherman at ITV (now known as Global), and co-host the highly-rated radio talk show "the Bill and Bill show" with Bill Jackson at radio station CJCA, and later on his own at station CHED

At the International Convention of Weathercasters, Scientists, and Environmentalists in Paris, France in 1995, Bill was awarded the International Excellence Award by his peers, for being the best on-air weatherman in the world.

Bill loved performing, and appeared or starred in more than 50 stage plays. He wrote a provincial-award winning play entitled: "Chinook". He even ran as a Liberal candidate in the Fort MacLeod riding in 1968. Bill devoted his time and energy to speaking at schools, universities and colleges, where he inspired many to consider the field of meteorology as a career choice.

Bill died in Lethbridge in 2006 of Alzheimer's and Parkinson's diseases. His papers, including the original manuscript of "A Year Down North" are in the Galt Museum and Archives in Lethbridge.

Made in the USA
Charleston, SC
05 February 2013